syndicate of sin: steamy mafia short stories

Syndicate of Sin

emilia rose

contents

mafia toy

PART 1

One million dollars per year.

That's how much the mafia boss and his wife offered me to be their toy. They wanted me to live in their home, sleep in their bed, and submit to them on my hands and knees at a moment's notice. The deal was to do whatever they wanted sexually and nothing more.

I nervously walked into the Buratti Family club, or more infamously known as The Syndicate, and to the back where the towering security guard in a black suit and black sunglasses stood with his fingers intertwined in front of his body. With their contract in my hand and my heart racing a million miles a second, I stared up at him.

"I'd like to see Constantino, please," I whispered.

After looking me up and down, he nodded and guided me to Constantino's office.

Of course, the money wasn't legal, and the job came with countless cons. If anyone found out about me, I'd be harassed by the cops, targeted by rival families, and seen as nothing more than a filthy, easy slut by the Buratti relatives.

But I'd be under Constantino's protection. And Constantino didn't take anyone's shit.

The guard knocked twice on Constantino's door. "Boss, Sage is here to see you."

"Sage?" Constantino asked from inside the room. "Send her in."

Staring down at my feet—I was far too nervous to make eye contact—I scurried into the room and sat down in front of Constantino, chewing on the inside of my lip. When the door clicked closed, I sucked in a breath and peeked a glance up at him.

Like the last time I saw him, he didn't smile when we made eye contact. Instead, he sat back in his chair and tapped his fingers on the armrest, glancing down at the contract in my shaky hands. "I see that you've come to a decision."

"Yes," I whispered.

He cleared his throat. "Speak up when you talk to me."

"Yes," I said louder, trying desperately to fake confidence.

Truth was that it scared me shitless. I didn't know how this was going to go. I had never been alone with him before and had only really spoken to his wife. She had been the one to sit next to me at the bar, to ask me for my number, and to propose this little deal.

"And?" he asked, an unreadable expression on his face.

"And I..." I fumbled with the contract and slid it across the desk. "I want to do it."

The corner of his lip twitched up as he grabbed the contract from me. "Do what?"

"I want to be your toy."

After a couple of moments of staring at me intensely, he flipped to the last page of the contract and cleared his throat. "Abele!" he shouted.

The security guard opened the door and stuck his head into the room. "Yes, sir?"

"Bring the car around the back."

When Abele disappeared, Constantino stood and held out his hand for me to take. "You will start tonight. Laila will be surprised and excited. She's been waiting for your reply since last Friday, Sage."

Hesitantly, I grabbed his hand. A rush of excitement shot through my body at the feel of him on my skin. This man must've held a gun in this hand so many times, used it to shoot and kill hundreds of people, and now… now he would use it to make me and his wife feel good together.

"And you?" I asked, finally having a bit of courage. "How do you feel about it?"

Guiding me toward the door, Constantino chuckled. "This might've been Laila's idea, but I've been waiting for your response almost as much as she has. Seeing how excited my wife was when she saw you last weekend, I can't wait to tie you up and have my way with both of you."

Heat rushed to my core, and I shifted slightly. I pressed my thighs together while we walked down the hall, away from the club and toward a back door. Abele opened the door for us, glancing briefly at our hands, and handed Constantino the keys.

"Don't call me for the night," Constantino said to Abele, opening the passenger side door. "Laila and I will be busy."

After curtly nodding at Constantino, Abele shut the back door. I slid into the passenger seat and pressed my hands to my thighs to stop them from bouncing, my nerves coming back. This was real now. Constantino was taking me back to his penthouse to become his and his wife's toy for however long an entire year.

Constantino drove about ten blocks down the busy NYC streets, then pulled into the underground parking lot to a skyrise. Nervously, I shuffled out of the car and walked with him to the elevators as he tapped on his phone.

"You will get half now," Constantino said, pressing the top button in the elevator. "Half once this year is complete. All your expenses will be paid, and you'll live in this building, a couple of floors down from us. We already have a place set out for you."

My phone buzzed, and an incoming message popped up from

my bank. A deposit of five hundred thousand dollars suddenly in my account. It was more than I thought I'd ever seen in my lifetime.

Shoving the phone back into my pocket, I glanced up at him. "Is that where we're going now?"

"No." He grabbed my hand and led me out of the elevator when the doors opened to the top floor. "We're going to see my wife."

Once he pressed his finger to the door pad and hit a couple buttons on his lock, the door swung open, and a shit-ton of nerves hit me all at once. Yet, instead of stepping back like I usually did, I walked into their penthouse and gulped.

It smelled just like her.

"Laila," Constantino called, his usual booming voice relatively calm now.

"In here!" Laila shouted from the backroom. "I've been waiting all day for you."

He placed a hand on my lower back and guided me down the hallway, toward a back room. A soft moan drifted down the hall, and I swallowed hard, the heat gathering between my legs. What would Laila do once she found me here? Did she even know I was coming?

When we reached the last door, I stopped in my tracks. Laila laid back on the bed in the sexiest pair of maroon lingerie I had ever seen, her eyes closed, her breasts barely covered, and her fingers dragging along her lacy panties that didn't cover anything.

"Look who I brought home for us, doll."

Laila opened her intense brown eyes and froze, sucking in sharply. For a moment, I thought that she would pull her hand away, but when her lips curled into a small smirk, she continued playing with her wet folds, the sight making me clench.

"What do you think?" Constantino asked, grabbing my hand and twirling me around like I was an object, but... I guess that's what I was to them now. The mafia's toy. To use. To play with. To pleasure themselves with.

"I love her," Laila murmured, biting her lower lip. "She's so sexy."

Suddenly, Constantino pulled me to him from behind, one arm coming around my waist, his other hand dipping between my legs to touch me under my skirt. I yelped in surprise, my heart pounding against my ribcage. He massaged my clit from behind, his other hand trailing up my body to gasp my breast through my top.

"Take it off of her," Laila said. "I've been waiting to finally see her."

With one of his hands still buried between my legs, Constantino pulled my shirt over my head and swiftly undid my bra, so my breasts bounced out of it. Laila spread her legs a bit further, hooking one finger around her panties and pulling it to the side so we could see everything as she rubbed herself.

After popping all of the buttons on my skirt, Constantino let it fall to the ground and left me in just my underwear. He continued to rub my pussy, the pressure building higher and higher in my core.

"Does my wife turn you on?" Constantino murmured into my ear.

"Yes," I breathed, watching as Laila's head lolled back as she moaned.

"Do you want to eat her pussy?"

A wave of heat rushed through me. "Yes."

Constantino slipped his fingers into my underwear and pulled apart my folds, teasing my pussy harder and faster until my legs trembled. "She's wanted to eat yours all week, kept asking me what you'd taste like."

After he pushed me closer to the bed, I placed my knees on the edge and let him continue. He gazed over my shoulder at his wife and gently kissed my shoulder. "Come over here, doll." He held out his wet fingers toward her. "Have a taste."

Laila crawled over to us, grabbed Constantino's wrist, and tugged his fingers into her mouth, wrapping her pink-painted lips around them like I'd imagine her sucking his cock, head bobbing back and forth slightly. Heat gathered between my legs.

Moving even closer to me, Laila placed her knees on either side of my thigh, sat her sopping pussy against my leg, and grinded herself against me, as she leaned over my shoulder to kiss her husband, her breasts in my face.

My breath caught in my throat, nerves zipping through me. I had never been with a woman before, but I had wanted to try it for so long. It wasn't a phase or taboo or even something impulsive. I had wanted to touch Laila since I had met her, because the way she looked at me made me hot all over.

Pushing my nerves to the side, I leaned forward and placed my mouth just above the hem of her lacy bra, kissing her softly at first. Laila placed her hand behind my head and pulled me closer to her, moaning into her husband's mouth and continuing to grind her pussy against my thigh.

Constantino shoved his fingers back into my panties, and Laila followed, her fingers moving just as quickly as her husband's. The sensations of two pairs of hands all over me drove me wild. I sucked harder on Laila's breast, tugging down her lacy bra and taking her nipple between my teeth.

"Fuck," Laila murmured, pulling away.

For a moment, I thought I had messed up or had done something wrong. But Laila pushed me down onto the bed with my back against the mattress and forced me to spread my legs. She and Constantino dipped their heads between my thighs and ate my pussy, each wanting to taste me for themselves.

The pressure rose in my core, my toes curling. "Oh, my gosh…"

Calloused hand gliding against my inner thigh, Constantino entered me with two fingers and pumped them in and out, his wife's tongue flicking against my swollen clit. I laced my hands into her hair, my legs trembling hard.

"I'm going to… to…" I threw my head back, on the verge of the most intense orgasm I have had in a while.

And when Laila said, "Come for me," and tugged on my nipple, I screamed out in pleasure. Wave after wave of ecstasy rushed through me, my arms and legs numbing in pins and needles.

If this was what the next year would bring, I would be so happy being their toy.

Once I finished, Laila sat back next to me. "Sit on my face," she said breathlessly, licking her bottom lip.

My brows furrowed together. "A-again?"

"Yes, again."

Hesitantly, I crawled onto her with my pussy in her face and her pussy in mine. I dipped my head to kiss just above her underwear line and clenched at the mere thought of me kissing her further down, yet the nerves reappeared because I had never done this before. Ever.

Wrapping her arms around my thighs, Laila spread my legs, pulled me down closer to her, and flicked her tongue against my clit. I dipped my head again and mirrored her actions, pulling off her underwear and flicking my tongue against her clit, just how I'd like.

She moaned against me, the vibration making me feel oh-so good.

Constantino watched hungrily, undoing his belt and pulling down his zipper. When he had kicked off his pants and pulled out his huge cock, he walked over to us and grabbed Laila's knees, pushing them as far apart as they could go, then slowly thrust into her cunt. In and out, he thrusted until I saw the juices covering his cock.

When he finally pulled out of her a couple moments later, he grasped my chin and forced me to look up at him. "Suck my wife's juices off my cock."

Clenching, I opened my mouth wide for him to enter me. Constantino shoved his huge cock down my throat and facefucked me until I cleaned his dick for him. When he finally pulled away, he pushed himself back into Laila and grunted. "Fuck, you both are so tight for me."

Constantino shifted from his wife, back to me, then to his wife. Over and over again.

Once he pulled away for good, he placed his hands on my waist and lifted me up with ease, turning me around so I faced Laila. She wrapped her arms around my shoulders, pulling me down to kiss her, softly at first but then wildly, like she was desperate for it.

With one knee on the bed, Constantino pushed his bare cock into me, grabbed my hips, and started pounding away. My breasts swayed against Laila's, her hands traveling down my body to cup them.

I moaned into her mouth, the pressure immediately rising in my core. Just when I was about to tip over the edge, Constantino pulled out of me and thrust himself into his wife. She moaned and kissed me harder, pinching and tugging on my nipples.

When her body tensed, Constantino pulled out of her and pushed himself back into me, teasing us both for the next ten minutes. Desperate for a release, I grinded my clit against her mound, the pressure rising higher and higher in my core.

"Oh, fuck," Laila breathed against me. "Keep doing that. You're going to make me come."

Not wanting to stop, I continued to grind myself against her while Constantino fucked me from behind. He dipped his hand and pushed a couple fingers into Laila's pussy, finger-fucking her at the same pace.

My toes curled, and I sucked on Laila's lower lip as wave after wave of pleasure rushed through me. Laila watched me come, her body tensing even harder, and then she finally threw her head back and came as Constantino stilled deep in my pussy.

When I collapsed on the bed beside Laila with her husband's cum deep in my cunt, she wrapped her arm around my waist and pulled me closer. "You're ours now, Sage. All ours."

Part 2

Dressed in a dark green lacy lingerie set, Laila laid on the bed beside me with her soft lips pressed against mine and her tongue moving rhythmically in my mouth. I pressed my thighs together to ease the ache between them and kissed her back, my hands traveling down the curves of her body.

Constantino had been at work all day, and Laila had been eyeing me like some kind of prey since her and her girlfriends got back to the high-rise apartment earlier to have an early brunch. To her friends, I was the housekeeper.

But we both knew that I didn't clean anything around this house.

The only thing we did together was make it dirty.

"God," Laila murmured against me. "I'm so glad that they're gone. I couldn't wait another moment to get you alone." She moved her hands down my body, undoing my bra and tugging it off me. "I haven't been able to stop thinking about you since last night with Constantino."

I dipped my fingers down her thigh and brushed them gently over her lacy panties, feeling how soaked they were for me. I whimpered into our kiss and crawled on top of her, trailing my mouth down her body until I reached the top of her panties.

She arched her back slightly and pulled off her underwear, tossing them over the bedside. When I placed my mouth on her cunt, I sighed in delight, my warm breath against her clit. I flicked my tongue over and over the sensitive bead and reached my hand between my thighs to rub myself off at the same time.

"Eat my pussy," Laila moaned, grasping my hair to hold me in place and bucking her hips back and forth to ride my face. "God, just like that, Sage. You're going to make me…" Her legs trembled around my shoulders, her pussy pulsing and moans escaping her lips. "Yes!"

Legs shaking, Laila cried out and came all over me. Then she flipped me over onto my back and crawled on top of me, pressing her lips against mine. Her tongue slipped into my mouth, her teeth gently biting down on my lower lip. She dipped a hand between my legs and rubbed my clit, her breasts swaying against mine.

"My turn," she said, kissing down my body, then burying her face between my legs. She placed my left leg on her shoulder and held the other apart and against the bed to spread them. Her tongue flicked out against my clit again, making me squirm.

Closing my eyes, I sank into the mattress and moaned softly, my hand laced in her hair.

"What do we have here?" Constantino asked.

I sucked in a surprised breath and snapped my eyes open. Constantino walked into the room, tugging off his tie, his gaze shifting from me to Laila who had pulled back from my cunt to look at her husband.

"Go back to eating her cunt, doll," Constantino commanded, unbuttoning his shirt, his dark eyes back on me. "I've had a long day at work. All I want to do is watch Sage squirm for you."

I laid back on the bed, my head on the pillows and my legs spread wide for Laila. She crawled closer up the bed toward me, on her hands and knees, stuck her ass up into the air, and dipped her head between my thighs. Fingers pulling my folds apart, she glided her tongue across my clit.

Constantino rested one knee on the bed behind Laila, his large hands all over her ass. He undid his pants and pulled out his cock, positioning himself at her entrance. When he pushed himself into her, she moaned against my clit

Every time that Constantino plowed into her from behind, her tits swayed against my thighs, her perky and hard nipples making me clench. I laced my hand into her hair and tugged on it to pull her closer to me, the pressure rising in my core.

"More," I whispered, arching my back.

God, I was close. So close.

"Don't cum," Constantino growled, fingers curling into Laila's hips.

"Come for me," Laila dared me, her fingers stroking my g-spot and her tongue flicking my clit back and forth and back and forth at just the right rhythm. "Don't listen to my husband. Come all over my face, Sage."

"If either of you cum, I'll fucking punish you for it."

"You're getting so tight for me," Laila murmured. "I know you want to."

"Laila," Constantino growled, grabbing a fistful of her hair and pulling her off my aching pussy. But her fingers were still inside me, thrusting in and out and vibrating the bundle of nerves that would soon make me explode.

"Are you disobeying me?" he continued, eyes hooded. "Do you need me to show Sage how I punish you to keep your filthy"–he wrapped his free hand around her chin–"little"–he stuck his fingers between her lips–"mouth in line?"

Laila stared down at me, brows drawn together in pleasure and continued moving her slender fingers inside my tightening hole. She knew that I wouldn't last much longer, that I would come all over her fingers in a couple moments.

"I'm going to come," she mouthed to me, big brown eyes wide, "when you do."

Unable to stop, I threw my head back as a leg-trembling orgasm ripped through my body. My chest moved up and down, my breaths quicker by the second. I grasped the bedsheets in my fists and pulled them up. Wave after wave of pleasure shot through my body.

Laila grinned wickedly down at me, then threw her head back and came on her husband. Our moans drifted through the large high-rise in the middle of the city. She pulled her fingers out of my cunt and stuck them into her mouth.

I relaxed against the mattress, wave after wave of pleasure rushing through me.

"I warned you," Constantino said, pulling out of her. Constantino tugged me up roughly with one hand and grabbed Laila in his other. With her wild hair all over the place, she shuffled beside him and glanced toward a room that neither of them had let me into since this little *thing* started.

Constantino stopped, pulled a key out of his pocket, and unlocked the door, pushing it open with the tip of his shoe, his cock still hard and swollen between his legs. As soon as he shoved us into the room, the dim lights turned on.

Thick chains and cuffs hung from each wall. My eyes widened slightly, taking in the toys on the dresser in the far corner of the room. Constantino brought me to one wall and locked the cuffs around each of my wrists and ankles, spreading me apart. Then did the same to Laila at the opposite wall.

"Your punishment will be worse than hers, doll," Constantino said, locking the cuffs around her wrists. He grabbed her jaw and forced her to look up at him. "The next time we go out, *I* will dress you. No wearing those expensive clothes. A brat like you gets fabric so cheap that all your little girlfriends will judge you for it."

To my surprise, Laila snapped her mouth shut and stared up at Constantino with wide eyes. I didn't know what had sparked her sudden change of action–I couldn't comprehend just how making Laila walk out of the house in a couple cheaper clothes could affect her so much–but it seemed like they exchanged a few private words with just their eyes.

Either the family was extremely judgemental... or something else had happened.

"Do you understand me?" Constantino asked, sharp jaw clenched.

"Yes," Laila whispered.

"Now," Constantino said, walking to a mahogany dresser and opening the first drawer. He pulled out two identical g-spot vibrators and walked back toward Laila, inserting one between her dripping pussy lips. "Since you both love to disobey, you'll stand here and watch each other cum over and over... and over again until I think you've had enough."

After securing the vibrator inside of her, Constantino walked over to me and drew the head of the vibrator across my swollen clit and to my entrance. My pussy was so wet that the vibrator slid right into me and filled me up.

I whimpered slightly, my nipples aching to me touched and tugged, and looked up at him, desperate for him to touch them, to touch *me*, any part of my body because I needed it so badly. "Please," I whispered.

Instead of giving me what I needed, he stepped back and stuffed his hand into his pocket, then he pulled out his phone and tapped a button on an app. My body jolted up, a strong vibration shooting through me.

Glancing over at Laila, I watched her naked body struggle against the cuffs and chains, her breasts bouncing slightly and her mouth parted in delight. Constantino shuffled backwards a few feet, then turned around and walked toward the door. "I'll be back in a few hours. Have fun girls."

Part 3

Constantino left Laila and me in his BDSM room, chained up to the walls with vibrators stuffed deep inside ourselves. I grasped the chains in my fists and clutched them tightly, pleasure rushing through me. We had been here for what must've been over an hour now, coming over and over again.

Every vibration from the toy thrust me higher and higher. I threw my head back and glanced at the wall length mirror on the side of the room, knowing that it probably wasn't a regular mirror, but a way for Constantino to watch us while we came, to control the vibrators and give or take away pleasure anytime he wanted.

My pussy tightened, and I moaned loudly. Wave after wave of pleasure rushed through my body from my core, making my limbs tingle and my mind numb. And while I would've taken the vibrator off my clit if I had control, the vibrations didn't stop.

In fact, every time I came, my vibrations seemed to get even faster somehow. Or maybe it just felt that way because they hadn't stopped for the longest damn time now. They had kept coming and coming, not once ceasing, not once slowing down.

"He's watching us," I breathed, glancing over at the puddle of cum underneath Laila. "Isn't he?"

Instead of looking over at the mirror, she stared at me and curled her lips into a soft smile. "Don't look over at him, Sage. Don't give him the satisfaction. You watch me as I come, then come with me," she said, body convulsing for a moment as I listened to her vibrations become louder. "Please, come with me."

Chained to the wall on the opposite side of the room, I stared at Laila who struggled against the restraints and for the first time, I really had the chance to admire her body. Dark brown hair that cascaded past her shoulders. Huge brown eyes that watched me as I watched her. Her breasts were bigger compared to her smaller frame, bouncing slightly every time a vibration shot through her.

"You're so fucking sexy," I whispered, pussy tightening on the vibrator for the umpteenth time in the past hour. All I wanted was to release another orgasm, let it shoot through my body and destroy me even further, but Laila wanted me to come with her. So I waited.

Laila intently watched my body, her eyes lingering on my swollen clit and sopping pussy.

The more she eyed me, the closer I came to orgasm.

I squeezed my eyes shut, praying that I wouldn't come too soon, hoping that I could hold out for just a bit longer. I clutched the chains between my fists again, legs trembling slightly. "Please, Laila, I don't know how much longer I can hold out. I'm about to come again."

"Not yet," she whispered, legs trembling. "Hold off. I'm so close, baby."

Just before Laila could give me permission to come, the door opened. Completely dressed in his suit, Constantino stepped into the room. Instead of paying any attention to his wife, he walked over to me and pulled the vibrator out of my pussy before I had the chance to come again.

He stepped to the side of me, so Laila could see everything that he was doing to me, then placed his fingers against my aching clit. My legs jerked into the air, my pussy clenching on nothingness and feeling so empty.

"Your clit is swollen, Sage," he murmured into my ear, gently moving his fingers around my clit. He pressed his hardness against the side of my thigh and growled into my ear lowly. "We're going to try this again. You're not going to come until *I* tell you that you can." With his free hand, he captured my nipple between two fingers. "Understand?"

"Yes," I breathed, legs shaking.

"I know my wife is sexy, but I'm the boss both inside and outside this bedroom." He gently sucked on the skin underneath my ear, his scruff tickling my neck. "You come when I tell you to from now on. Not her."

Desperately trying to hold back my orgasm, I nodded. "Okay."

"Watch my wife," he murmured, tugging on my nipple and making me moan softly. Laila was watching her husband skillfully touch my folds. "She's going to come for me on command, then you'll learn to do the same thing."

I swallowed hard and stared at his side-profile, unable to believe that I was really here with a mafia boss and his wife. Out of all the women in the world that they could've had, they chose me. They *wanted* me.

He turned back to me, lip curling into a smirk. His eyes were as dark as I imagined they'd be when he was holding a gun to someone's head, threatening to pull the trigger, and killing them dead.

"Doll," Constantino called, his dark gaze still focused on me. "Come."

On command, Laila threw her head back and screamed louder than I ever heard her. Body convulsing, she tugged on the chains and cried out in pleasure, drawing her legs together as much as she could.

Pleasure coursed through my body at the mere sight of her. My pussy tightened, and I squeezed my eyes closed, forcing myself to take steady breaths so I wouldn't explode all over Constantino's fingers.

"Please," I whispered to him. "Can I come?"

There was a moment of complete silence.

"Open your eyes, and look at me."

I opened my eyes and stared into that cold and calloused gaze. "Please."

"No."

Pressure rose even higher in my core. I dug my fingernails into my palm and whimpered. He stepped back from me and walked over to Laila, taking out her vibrator, undoing his belt, then pulling out his cock. Once he undid the chains around her ankles, he lifted her legs into the air and positioned himself against her entrance.

When he slipped himself inside her, I whimpered again. I didn't even have a vibrator inside me anymore, but just watching him fuck her was pushing me closer and closer to the edge, and I didn't know how much longer I would be able to last.

"Oh, god," Laila moaned.

He pounded into her tight hole, his cock becoming wetter and wetter with every thrust.

"Cover my dick in your cum, doll," he commanded Laila, tucking some hair behind her ear. "So I can push it into our little toy who's convulsing over there and make her feel good." He grasped her jaw and forced her to look at me. "Look at her struggling, on the brink of coming."

He stuck three fingers into her mouth, the same fingers that were playing with me. She sucked on his fingers, her saliva dripping down her chin. "Please," she begged him. "God, please, let me come. She tastes so good."

After he stuck his fingers deeper into her mouth, he whispered something into her ear that I couldn't hear. Then she threw her head back and came while staring at me, spit rolling off her parted lips.

Once her body slowly relaxed, Constantino pulled out of her and walked over to me. He took off the chains around my ankles and grasped my hips, pulling me toward him and positioning himself at my entrance.

"Beg for my cock covered in my wife's cum."

I stared down at Laila's thick juices covering his throbbing cock, his head centimeters from my entrance. My core tightened even more, and I whimpered again, desperate to come on him too. "Please, give it to me, Constantino. Please, I need it."

He grasped my hips and shoved himself into me hard one time. "Come."

I parted my lips, wanting to scream out loud, but the pleasure was almost too much to bear. My legs trembled uncontrollable, as I came all over his cock in the first thrust. Wave after wave of ecstasy rushed through me.

Contantino pulled out of me, unhooked his wife from her chains, and forced her to drop to her knees. "If Sage tastes so good, suck her off me," he commanded. She wrapped her mouth around his dick and sucked me off him, cheeks drawn in tightly.

He wrapped his hand through her hair and shoved himself as deeply as he could get. He threw his head back and grunted deeply, hips convulsing. When he finally came, he pulled out of her and undid my restraints.

"Have you girls learned your lessons?" he asked.

My lips curled into a soft smile, and I glanced over at Laila who had the same smirk on her face. I guessed that we hadn't, and the only thing left to do was have him teach us again.

Part 4

Monday night, I laid back on the memory-foam mattress next to Laila. She buried her face into the crook of my neck and sucked on my sensitive skin, then purred, her teeth gliding against the fragile column. "You're so fucking sexy," she murmured.

All day, I had to listen to Laila's best friend, Bethany, make snide comments toward her and act as if she was the best fucking friend in the world. Lately, she had been around way too much, and I hadn't gotten any time alone with Laila.

So, when we got a few moments, we were both going to take advantage of it.

I moaned softly and arched my back, my hands gliding up the curves of her body, then grabbed one of her breasts, squeezing lightly. She peppered kisses to my mouth and kissed me, her tongue slipping between my lips.

Constantino walked into the room, his tie already loosened around his neck and a glass of sambuca in his hand. He took a sip and watched us with dark and curious eyes, full lips curled up into a half-smirk.

"You girls," he growled, placing his drink down on a shelf and pulling off his tie.

Laila pulled away from me to glance over at her husband, then sank a hand between my legs to gently rub my clit. Constantino stalked over to us both and crawled up onto the bed after pulling off his shirt.

"You've skipped dinner with the family," he said to Laila.

Laila arched her back as he kissed her neck, his stubble rubbing against the sensitive skin. She shivered and glanced over at me, intertwining her fingers with me on the bed. "I had my hands full," she said.

But that wasn't the reason, and we both knew it.

For as long as I'd been their *help*–at least, that's what the family thought I was–I hadn't been able to figure Laila out. She had a love-hate relationship with the family, and I couldn't figure out the reason for it.

It wasn't the violence.

It wasn't the people… at least, I didn't think it was. She had best friends in the family that she'd go out with every other day. Bethany was an absolute bitch, but they still hung out together. Could it be her, maybe the others?

But sometimes, Laila would purposefully miss dinners or get nervous when Constantino said something to her about them. She couldn't fear them. She fucking lead the mafia with the most dangerous man in this city.

"What's got you all tense?" she murmured against my skin. "Relax, Sage. Let me touch you. I haven't been able to see you for the past few nights. Bethany has taken up all of my time lately with this gala that she wants to host."

I hated the mere sound of her name more and more every single time it rolled off Laila's tongue. Bethany was her best friend in this family, but she was so fake, always trying to convince Laila that she needed to get lip fillers more often, needed to have a different hairstyle every damn week, or needed to get plastic surgery to *look better*.

I didn't give a fuck about that stuff. Laila could do what she wanted with her body. I just hated that Bethany the Bitch had to make her feel less like herself. Laila would never admit that Bethany made her feel that way, but I could tell.

It was just something that I could pick up on.

Maybe I was just being a salty, jealous bitch, because Laila spent more time with her than she did me, and maybe… I was getting too close to Laila *and* Constantino, which was not in the contract.

All we agreed upon was me being their toy in exchange for one million dollars.

Not feelings.

After I forced myself to relax, Laila kissed down my neck again and continued to rub my pussy until it glistened with juices. I moaned and spread my legs a bit wider to give her better access. She was building me higher, quicker than she ever had.

I squeezed Laila's hand harder, intertwining my fingers with hers and pushing away my developing feelings. To her, I was just a toy. I wasn't a friend or a lover or the help. A simple toy she could use with her husband to get off.

Constantino sprawled a hand over each of our stomachs, forcing us to lie down next to each other. Once he crawled up toward us, he stuck his thumbs into our mouths to wetten them. Then he snaked his hands down our bodies to our pussy.

At the same time, he sunk three fingers in both of us and placed his thumbs on our clits, rubbing torturous circles against us as his fingers worked magic. I arched my back slightly, my pussy tightening around his fingers and the pressure building higher.

Laila squeezed my hand, and I glanced over at her. She stared at me with huge, lustful eyes and leaned over to place a hot and heated kiss right on my lips. When she slipped her tongue into my mouth, I clenched around Constantino.

"You girls both just got so tight for me," he growled, curling his fingers faster over my g-spot. He leaned over and laid hot, wet kisses from Laila's breasts to my own, gently tugging one of my nipples between his teeth. "You love playing with her, doll, don't you?"

Laila moaned into my mouth, her fingers tightening around mine and her tongue moving faster. I clenched even harder, focusing on the immense pleasure building in my core. All Constantino had to do was…

Laila pushed at my entrance with two of her fingers and shoved them into me too. When she got deep, Constantino flicked my g-spot with his middle finger, and I arched my back and came on him. My body seized beside Laila, her kisses doing nothing but tipping me even harder over the edge. My pussy pulsed on his fingers.

Once I had come down from my high, Constantino pulled his fingers from my pussy and seized Laila's waist to lift her. He turned her around and placed her on top of me, so she straddled my waist and her pussy laid flat on my stomach.

Constantino grabbed the backs of my thighs to pull us to the edge of the bed and to spread them wide. "Arch your back, doll," he ordered Laila as she lowered her chest until it touched mine and pushed her hips further back. "And rub that clit against Sage's."

Heat rushed through my core. A moan slipped out of my lips as Laila bucked her hips back and forth, her pussy against mine and her nipples gliding against my chest. It drove me higher and higher, pushing me closer to the edge right to the brink of another orgasm.

When Constantino pushed himself inside me, I cried out in pleasure and captured one of Laila's nipples between my teeth, sucking on her breasts. She threw her head back and moaned. Constantino released one of my legs and wrapped his large hand around the front of her throat, placing his mouth on hers.

He pushed into me over and over and over, sending me closer to the edge, and then he moaned into Laila's mouth and stuck a few fingers into her pussy. She continued to grind her pussy against mine, the friction making me feel so fucking good.

Suddenly, Laila stiffened and screamed out. Her body trembled against mine, her hips bucking unintentionally and sending me over the edge once more. Constantino stilled inside me, gently biting down on his wife's shoulder but his dark gaze focused on me as we all came.

When Laila collapsed on top of me, Constantino pulled out and picked his wife off the bed to set her on her feet. She clutched onto him tightly and pressed her thighs together the way I did after I came and couldn't handle coming again right away.

"Let's get you girls cleaned up," Constantino said, helping Laila to the bathroom.

I stayed in bed. "I'm going to… hang back for a while. Maybe some other time."

They never invited me into the bathroom to get cleaned up after sex. Usually, I left right away because they got intimate later. And by intimate, I meant Constantino would hold Laila the way that I wanted him *and* her to hold me too.

I didn't want to see it, because it hurt.

But tonight, I couldn't seem to pull my clothes back on and leave the room. I sat on the bed and listened to Laila giggling in the shower with her husband. Part of me felt so jealous about this whole situation, and the other part of me couldn't stop the hot tears from piling up in my eyes from what I witnessed today.

Bethany had been so mean to Laila, but Laila had brushed it off. I didn't know why Laila kept her around, but she didn't seem like she had many friends. At least, not many real ones. And for some ungodly reason, it seemed like Laila *wanted* acceptance from Bethany.

I couldn't understand it. It hurt so badly to watch.

After curling up into a ball, I grabbed the bedsheets and wrapped them around my body. My chest was tight, and I was trying hard not to cry. I was trying so fucking hard, but being an empath sucked sometimes.

The bathroom door opened, and Laila stepped out of the room.

"Laila," I whispered, tears pricking the corners of my eyes.

God, what was wrong with me?

"Sage," Laila said, wrapping a silky robe around her small frame and hurrying over to me. Steam rolled out of the bathroom as

Constantino opened the door and leaned out to see what happened. "What's wrong? Why are you upset?"

Knowing that I would never be anything more than a toy to them, I pushed away the tears and forced the fakest damn smile. "Nothing is wrong," I lied. "That was just so intense for me. I..." I swallowed hard, my mouth parched, and turned to exit the room. "I need some rest."

Before I could make it far, Laila seized my wrist and stopped me. "You're lying."

I opened my mouth to argue with her, but no words would come out. Tears filled my eyes again, and I hated the fact that I cared too much. One of my reservations about agreeing to their proposal was that I caught feelings too quickly.

It was so stupid to agree to it.

"What's wrong?" Constantino asked, pulling a towel over his naked body. Beads of water from the shower rolled down his muscular chest and soaked into the towel. "Did I hurt you?" he asked, surprisingly concerned too.

A guy like him, who killed people ruthlessly, shouldn't care.

"Nothing is wrong," I repeated to convince my own self to stop with the damn tears.

"Don't lie to me," Constantino said, voice hardening the way it did with Laila the last time we all had sex together, the way I had heard it while he talked on the phone to his men and wanted something done. It terrified me.

I didn't *want* to lie to him, because I didn't want any punishment either.

So, I turned to Laila and frowned. "Why do you listen to Bethany?"

"What'd Bethany say?" Constantino asked, concerned.

"All she does is make snide comments," I whispered. "About how Laila should do her makeup a certain way, get lip fillers, try out plastic surgery. She doesn't stop, and it fucking hurts to watch."

"Maybe that's what *I* want," Laila said.

But she was lying. She didn't want someone to constantly put her down. Nobody did.

"Then that's fine, but… I just…"

"You just, what?" Laila asked, crossing her arms and suddenly becoming defensive. Her strong gaze seemed to falter for a moment, then she looked down at her feet and pressed her lips together, voice softer this time. "Why are you commenting on the way I look? I thought you loved it."

"I do, Laila," I said.

I didn't know how to articulate something like this without looking like a fool who had started falling for a married couple. I just wanted her to feel beautiful the way she was, and if she wanted to change it, then she could make that decision herself, *and not with her best friend shoving it down her throat.*

"Then, what does Bethany have to do with any of this?" she said, becoming more defensive than I had ever seen her. "Are you jealous of her?"

This time, I dropped my gaze to my feet. My mouth was so dry, my cheeks flaming hot. I wanted to curl up into a ball and cry my eyes out after what I witnessed today and after this stupid thing that I had to make into an argument.

"No," I said, pulling on my clothes and refusing to make eye contact with her.

But I was so damn jealous of Bethany, because Laila talked about her all the time and admired Bethany's looks, and I felt so ugly compared to her. Sometimes I really did feel like *the help*, because if Bethany was the kind of girl that Laila really enjoyed, then I was nothing.

"I'm just exhausted," I lied again, hurrying past Laila out of the room and to the front door. "I really need to sleep. I'm just… I'm just saying things that aren't true." Another lie. "I'll see you both whenever you need me."

Before I could escape their high-rise, Laila grabbed my wrist again. "Wait, Sage, I--"

Yet I couldn't stay here any longer. I couldn't or else I'd ball my eyes out and confess all my feelings for her. So, I pulled my wrist out of her strong hold and shuffled out the front door. "I'm sorry. Goodnight."

These one-shots have been turned into a book. Read Mafia Toy now!

mafia daddy

"Come on, Daddy," I said, sitting in a bath already filled to the brim with bubbles and drizzling more into the tub by the second.

"You know that I don't take bubble baths, sweetheart," he said, leaning against the sink counter with his arms crossed over his chest and his dark, devilish eyes focused on me. He had on a blue button up shirt with the sleeves rolled up his tattooed forearms and gray suit pants that fit him a bit too perfect, especially around the crouch.

I placed the bottle of bubbles down beside me and sank into the tub, pulling and pushing the bubbles away with my hands. "Please," I pleaded, gently biting down on my lower lip and giving him the eyes I knew he couldn't resist.

He drew his tongue across his top teeth, staring me down like a hungry predator, and tugged on his tie. "If you keep splashing around like that, I might think about it." His gaze dropped to my tits covered in bubbles.

Heat gathered in my core at the mere sight of that man. It was the first night he's been home for who knew how long. It was always business, business, business with him being the boss, but I wanted him to join me for the night. Just one.

If he was at work right now, blood would cover his hands, be splattered on his face, and drip down his nice button-up shirt. Something about being with a man so feral, so ruthless... it did something to me. Something it shouldn't.

"Come on," I said, sitting back and toying with my nipples just under the bubbles.

His gaze lingered, his tongue gliding against his bottom lip now. He was hungry.

"Play with me," I begged, letting one hand slip even lower to between my legs. "Let me show you what I do every night while you're gone, killing any man who even looks in my direction the wrong way."

A low growl came from his throat, and he pulled off his tie, then let it slide from his hands and onto the tiled floor. He undid the first button on his shirt, his graying brown hair glistening under the dim light.

"I should be at work."

"But you're going to fuck your little girl instead," I said, desperate for him to slid his huge dick inside me already. I shifted in the water, sitting on my knees with my breasts still covered in suds, and added more bubble bath into the tub. "I'll put more bubbles in for you too."

"No more of this," he said, grabbing the plastic container from my hand and placing it on the sink counter. With his body still turned, he let his shirt slide off his shoulders, revealing his muscular and tattooed back. "You have enough bubbles in there for three baths."

"But Daddy," I said, grinding my hips back and forth to feel some friction–any friction–on my clit. It had been aching so badly for hours now, and he had told me not to even think about touching myself. If I didn't, he said he'd stay home with me tonight.

Let's just say that I had been way too worked up throughout the day.

He turned back around and undid his belt, then placed his gun on the counter beside the bath. I sat up taller, reaching for his pant button and getting suds all over him as I undid it. I didn't care though. All that mattered was that he was mine tonight.

My gaze lingered on his cock, hard and hanging between his legs. He was built like a fucking bull, his dick long, thick, and veiny. I pressed my thighs together, remembering the feeling of this morning when his balls were slapping against my clit as he fucked me doggy.

After kicking off his pants, he stepped into the tub behind me and sat. Some water and suds sloshed over the edge. He pulled me back toward him, his hand coming around my throat and his mouth against my ear.

"You're the only woman I would ever do this for," he growled. "Do you understand me?"

"Yes, Daddy," I whispered.

"Say it," he said, voice tense.

"I'm the only woman that you would ever do this for."

"Good girl," he praised, grabbing my hair and tugging back on it. He placed his lips on the crook of my neck and sucked gently on the skin, sending shivers down my spine. "You were a good girl today too, weren't you?"

"Yes, Daddy."

"What didn't you do?"

"I didn't touch myself for the entire day. Not once."

He sank a hand between my legs and rubbed my clit. "I bet you wanted to, huh?"

I whimpered and laid back against him, his hard cock right against my ass. Then, I spread my legs as far as they would go in this bathtub to give him better access. "I wanted to so badly. I couldn't stop thinking about this morning."

"That's because you're my horny…" He rubbed me faster. "… little…" Faster. "… whore."

My legs trembled slightly, and I whimpered again, my tits bouncing around the bubbles. He looked over my shoulder down at them, pulled his hand away from my aching clit, and rested his hands underneath my tits, bouncing them up and down in the bubbles.

"Show me what you do every night in the bathtub while I'm working," he said. "I want to see just how desperate you can get, so while I'm at the club, killing people *for you*, I know what I get to come home to. Can you do that for me, sweetheart?"

After whimpering again–because, god, I loved his filthy mouth and the way he touched me–I pushed my hand between my legs and around my folds. My clit was so sensitive that the moment I touched it, my body jerked into the air.

He kneaded my tits, every now and then tugging on my nipples, so I knew who I belonged to, so I knew that he was still here ready to give me the best dick I ever had in my life. I rubbed my clit harder and faster in anticipation.

"Is that all you do, sweetheart?" he asked, his voice almost condescending. He pulled my hand away from my clit and placed both my hands on my breasts. "Let me show you how I'd touch you every night if I was home."

Instead of rubbing my clit, he shoved his fingers between my folds and into my pussy. I threw my head back, moaned, and tightened around him. All I wanted was for him to be inside me already. I could feel his dick twitching against my ass.

"You're going to do everything that I say, Sweetheart," he said. "Understand?"

"Yes, Daddy."

"Good girl," he cooed into my ear, beginning to pound his fingers into me. The heel of his palm smacked against my clit each time. "Because you know that I would do anything for you, even kill a man who tried to flirt with you. You're mine, sweetheart. All mine."

The pressure rose in my core. I squeezed my eyes closed and nodded, trying so desperately to hold back an orgasm, but it was coming on strong. I could feel it as I waited for him to tell me to come. The last time I didn't wait, he punished me.

"Tug on your nipples," he said, sliding a third finger into me.

I took my nipples between my soapy fingers and pulled, another moan escaping my lips.

"Harder."

I pulled harder as he finger-fucked me, his mouth sucking on the column of my neck, no doubt leaving a large hickey for all his men to see tomorrow.

"Harder."

I pinched down harder on the sensitive buds and pulled, a wave of pleasure rushing through me and building me higher and higher. More heat gathered between my trembling legs, and I tightened on him.

"Don't come," he ordered.

But I was so close. So fucking close.

"Please," I begged, knowing that I would tip over the edge soon.

"No."

"Please, Daddy," I pleaded. "I'm begging you."

"No," he said, voice harder this time, the way I only heard it while he was working.

After snapping my mouth closed, I pulled my knees to my chest and tried hard to knock myself down from the high I was about to be in. All he had to do was flick his palm against my clit one last time and I would–

He slammed his fingers into me, and I cried out but somehow, someway, held myself from the earth-shattering orgasm lingering deep within my core. He smirked against my neck and praised me for being a good girl and holding myself together.

Then he pulled his fingers from me, turned me around in the water, so I faced him, and made me straddle his waist. Once he positioned himself at my entrance, he grasped my hips and pulled me down onto him.

"Come."

One single word, and my body reacted. I grasped tightly onto his shoulders, my fingers digging into his back, my legs trembling, and my head thrown back. Cries escaped my lips. Waves of pleasure rolled through me.

I bounced on his cock, not caring that the water was sloshing over the edge of the tub. He leaned forward and kissed me hard, his fingers digging into my ass as he pulled me down on him over and over.

"You're mine," he growled again, grunting against me. "All mine."

"Yours, Daddy. I'm yours."

He slammed me down on him one last time and stilled, his body tensing then relaxing all within a couple moments. I continued to bounce on him until all his cum was buried deep inside me. Then I slowed and pulled him out of me, sinking down into the tub in front of him.

"Thank you," I said, relief washing through my body. "For staying home with me tonight. I know that you have a lot of work to do and I don't want to hold you back from anything, but..." I crawled up near him again and wrapped my arms around his shoulders. "This means a lot to me."

"Anything for you," he mumbled against my lips, arms resting on the sides of the tub. He grazed his finger across his gun, smirked, and repeated, "Anything for you."

Part 2

"Where are we going?" I asked, gazing out the tinted car windows at all the New Yorkers and tourists walking down the streets in a large pack. We were headed through Times Square at peak hour.

"Take off your clothes, sweetheart," Daddy said.

"My... my clothes?" I whispered, gulping. "All of them?"

"All of them."

When we pulled up to a redlight, I took another nervous glance out the window. So many people walked down the streets, the cops lined up at every corner. Even with these tinted side windows, someone would definitely see me through the windshield.

"But..."

Daddy grasped my jaw and forced me to look over at him. His eyes were as dark as the night sky above us, as dark as I imagined them to be when he executed another man for screwing him over.

"Now."

Pressing my thighs together, I began tugging off my clothes. Button by button, I undid my shirt and let it slide off my shoulders. Tourists walked across the crosswalk, but Daddy made me stare at him as I undid my bra and let my breasts bounce out of it.

"Good girl," he cooed, drawing his thumb across my bottom lip. "Now your skirt."

After shimmying out of my skirt and thong, I sat completely naked in the passenger seat of his car. While he had on the heat, my nipples were hard and aching for him to touch them. The light turned green, and I pulled my gaze away from him and toward the road.

"Turn toward me, put your back on the seat, and spread your legs apart for me, sweetheart," Daddy said, driving much slower than usual as if he *wanted* every single person in the city to see me. "Let me see your pretty pussy."

I shuffled my feet together and whimpered, not wanting my full pussy on display for anyone other than him. But I couldn't stop myself from following every one of his orders and commands.

So, I slipped down in the seat, turned toward him, and wrapped my arms underneath the backs of my legs to spread them apart as much as I could. He pulled his gaze away from the road for a moment and glanced down at my pussy, grunting softly under his breath.

"Fuck, sweetheart," he growled, pressing a hand over the growing bulge in his suitpants.

"Like this, Daddy?"

With one hand wrapped tightly around the steering wheel–making every one of his muscles flex through his button-up shirt, he reached over with his other hand and gently rubbed my clit. "Just like this."

I whimpered, the pressure building in my core quickly, and

spread my legs wider. I loved pleasing Daddy. I loved when he touched me, when he looked at me with nothing but uncontrollable lust in those dark eyes.

When we pulled up to another stoplight, I tensed. "You should… you should stop. Someone is going to see."

"Nobody is going to see you, sweetheart." He rubbed me even harder. "And if they do, then I'll have to take care of them, because *nobody* gets to see you like this–my perfect, desperate, little cumslut–except me."

More heat gathered between my legs, my heart pounding inside my chest as a cop car pulled up next to us. I pressed my thighs together and stared behind him with wide eyes. "But there are police. They're going to–"

"Spread your legs."

His voice was low and terrified me to my very core. It was nothing like I heard from him before, and I found myself immediately pulling my legs apart again even though I knew that if the cops took one single glance through the windows, they'd see us. Hell, they've been trying to find a reason to arrest him for months now.

"Daddy," I whined.

Instead of answering my whimpers and whines, he slipped two fingers inside me and started pumping them in and out of my sopping pussy. The pressure rose in my core, my entire body becoming overwhelmingly hot and bothered.

"Please," I begged, pushing on his hand. "Daddy…"

After shoving another finger inside me, he stilled them deep in my pussy. "Do you trust me, sweetheart?"

"Yes, but–"

"Let go of my hand," he ordered. "Before I roll my window down and really let them see you."

"But you said that you won't let anyone see me…" I started breathlessly, my pussy tightening around his fingers and desperate for him to start pumping them in and out of me again. "… naked."

"Nobody gets to see you naked and lives," he said, thrusting his fingers hard and fast inside me. "If you make me roll down this window, because you won't stop whining, then I'll have to kill them, sweetheart. All for you."

Not wanting anyone else to die because of me–because I knew that he would run these cops off the road, end their lives, and make it look like a rival family did it–I pulled my hand away from his and let him have me.

He owned every single inch of my pussy anyway, and he knew it too.

As the light turned green, he hit the gas and drove ahead of the officers, one hand on the steering wheel and the other buried deep inside me. We drove through the streets of New York City, between hundreds of skyscrapers and tens of thousands of people, the moonlight and the city lights shining in through the window.

I grasped onto the seats, my legs beginning to tremble uncontrollably. "Please, Daddy."

"Please, what, sweetheart?"

"Please, can I come?"

"I'm not done playing with your tight little hole yet."

Toes curling, I squeezed my eyes closed and moaned. I wouldn't be able to hold out much longer. My nipples were aching. My pussy was tight around his fingers, gripping them harder each time like I didn't want him to pull his three fingers out of me.

"Harder, Daddy!" I moaned. "Harder!"

He grunted, pounding his fingers faster and harder into me, curling them at just the right angle to hit my g-spot. Every. Single. Time. My legs trembled harder and faster. I was about to tip over the edge.

"Daddy, I'm so close," I breathed, trying desperately to take steady breaths. "Please."

"Come for Daddy, sweetheart."

I threw my head back against the seat and screamed out loud. Pleasure shot through my body, making every single bit of me tingle in ecstasy. Wave after wave washed through me, my mind completely fuzzy and numb.

Once he finally pulled his fingers out of me, he stuck them into his mouth, sucked off all the juices, and continued driving through the busy city. I took a deep breath and scrambled to sit up straight, still completely naked in his car.

When we pulled up to another redlight, we sat behind another police car. One of the officers rolled down his window, hung his arm out it, and glanced at me through the rearview mirror, his lips curled into an ugly, evil smirk.

Daddy caught him staring at my naked body and tightened his hand around the steering wheel. "Buckle your seatbelt, sweetheart. We have a couple people to take care of tonight."

mafia menage

With his hands bound behind his back, a blindfold wrapped around his eyes, and his body duct taped to our kitchen chair, I stared at the man who vied for my cold, dark heart. Milo really knew how to get under my skin. Now, it was my turn to get underneath his.

"Take off the blindfold," I commanded Verano.

Verano pulled the blindfold off my husband. Milo struggled against the restraints, shouting something in Italian at me, but I didn't give a fuck what he was saying. I didn't even care if he was apologizing for flirting with that whore the other night.

This was payback.

"You want to flirt with other girls in your clubs?" I asked Milo, feeling no sympathy.

He might've been the mafia boss and my husband for the past two years, but I wasn't going to take any shit from him. If he got to flirt with other girls, then I got to fuck the strongest, sexiest body guard that he assigned to protect me in front of him. And, God, I would enjoy it.

"Payback's a bitch," I said, kissing my husband on the mouth and walking backward toward the bed. When my legs hit the back of the bed, I crawled up onto the mattress, laid back, and curled my pointer finger at Verano. "Come and eat my pussy, V," I said to him, spreading my legs and staring at Milo.

That man would come to his senses tonight. He would know not to *look* at another girl again. I didn't care how many whores tried to throw themselves at him for his money. He was mine. *Only mine.*

"I swear to fucking god, Verano," Milo said between gritted teeth. "Don't fucking touch her, or I'll kill you in your fucking sleep tonight."

"No, you won't," I said, tilting my head. "Because this is what *you* should've been doing every night you were at *work* with all those girls in your club. You should've been the one between my legs, eating my cunt, and fucking me in your bed."

Verano crawled between my legs, eyeing my pussy like he was hungry for another man's dinner.

Ever since I married Milo, Verano hadn't been able to keep his eyes off me. I had caught him checking me out every time I stepped out of the pool or stripped out of my clothes in Milo's club. And at first, I ignored those hungry glances.

That was until I found out that Milo was fucking around.

"This isn't the first time," I said to Milo.

Verano moved his tongue in small, circular motions around my clit, driving me higher.

"What do you mean that this isn't the first time?" Milo gritted out.

"Last weekend, after you passed out drunk on our bed, I snuck him into our bedroom and made him fuck me over the side of the bed as you slept." I pulled Verano's face closer to my cunt and bucked my hips back and forth, my fingers slipping into his thick black hair. "God, I don't know how you didn't wake up. He was fucking me so hard that the bed frame was shaking."

"Lara," Milo growled at me. "You better watch your fucking mouth."

"Or what?" I asked, batting my lashes. "Are you going to fuck my mouth while you're tied up? How about Verano does, instead?

I'm sure that he wouldn't mind being inside me again, would you, V?"

Verano growled against my pussy, then crawled off me and grabbed my throat in his large hand, shoving me down to the hardwood floors. After he pulled off his belt and undid his pants, he whipped out his huge, hard cock and pressed it against my lips.

I stared at Milo as Verano plunged into my throat, forcing me to take his cock inch by inch until every bit of him was inside me. My eyes watered slightly, and I couldn't help gagging on him. Instinctively, I pulled my head back to breathe, but Verano held me closer.

"You love being my little slut," Verano growled down at me, roughly pushing a thumb across my saliva-covered lower lip. "Don't you?"

With his cock still buried deep inside my throat, I stared up at him to give him my full attention and nodded. When he pulled out of me, he stuck his fingers deep in my mouth to gag me again. Then he rubbed his saliva-covered fingers across my face, smearing my makeup.

"Please," I begged, like a hungry whore, deciding to ignore a furious Milo. "I want you inside me. Fill me with your cum."

"Lara!" Milo shouted at me.

Verano pulled me to my feet and tossed me onto the bed. I pulled him down next to me, my entire body aching for him to be inside me again. The last few times, we had to sneak around Milo, but now...

My pussy tightened at the thought of how hard Milo would fuck me after I finished with his guard. How desperate he'd be to prove himself to me. How incredibly dark and rough he would get with us both.

Verano laid back on the bed, and I crawled toward him on my hands and knees, my hips swaying from side to side to give Milo a show. Once I made it up to Verano, I straddled his waist in a reverse cowgirl position, so I could watch Milo watch us.

"You're going to watch your most trusted man betray you," I said to my husband, hovering over Verano's cock. With one hand on

Verano's chest behind me, I used my free hand to guide his cock to my entrance and made it wet with my juices. "All he has to do is slip it in."

Before Milo could say anything, Verano grasped my hips and pulled me down onto him. His cock filled my tight hole, pushing deeper and deeper inside of me and stretching out my walls. I threw my head back against him and let out a moan, the pleasure rushing through me.

"Oh, God," I moaned.

"I fuck her every night," Verano said, hand around my throat. He pumped into me, sucked on the crook of my neck, and stared up at me, his dark eyes like the devil in this light. "She's a nasty, desperate whore who's hungry for cock. I tried to stay away from her, but I couldn't fucking hold myself back from her sexy little body anymore."

"More," I begged, staring down at him. "More, please."

Verano wrapped one arm around my waist and gently rubbed my clit.

I glanced over at Milo who glared at us and desperately tried to escape the restraints, but he wasn't getting out. I had made sure to tie him up extra good, just the way he showed me how he restrained one of the men who betrayed him when we first started dating.

"Harder!" I cried, pussy tightening around Verano. "Please, fuck me harder!"

"Stop it!" Milo shouted at us. "When I get out of here, I'm going to kill you, Verano."

"Don't worry, Milo. He hasn't come inside me yet." I continued to buck my hips up and down on V's cock, pushing us both closer to the edge. "I refused to let him come inside me every other time. I wanted to take his cum for the first time while you were watching us. I wanted to show you just how much of him is inside me."

"Lara!"

"Fill me, Verano!" I pleaded. "Oh, god! Please, it'll make me come."

Verano slammed his fat cock deep into my pussy and stilled. My body spasmed on his, my pussy quivering and milking out his thick cum. I wanted every last drop of him inside me, sinking deep inside my cunt, so when he pulled out, Milo could see.

Because I wasn't letting Milo off *that* easily.

"Please, Verano," I begged. "I stopped taking birth control weeks ago."

Verano shuddered and grunted underneath me, pushing me over the edge. My legs trembled on either side of him, my pussy quivering again on his fat cock. I dug my fingers into the bedsheets and came hard.

Wave after wave of pleasure shot through me. *I fucking love this.*

After crawling off Verano's lap, I sauntered over to Milo who still struggled against his restraints. I straddled his lap, taking a fistful of his hair and pulling it back. "Oh, baby, stop struggling. You have me forever. No matter which other man puts his dick inside my pussy."

"You're mine," Milo growled at me, eyes rageful. "*Mine.*"

I undid his pants and pulled out his *hard* cock, then hovered over it. Verano's cum leaked out of my pussy and onto my husband's cock. "Do you like when I fuck other guys in front of you, my *dearest* husband? Hm?"

"If you don't let me go now, you're not going to like your punishment."

"Punishment?" I giggled, letting the last of Verano's cum drip out of me, then dropping to my knees in front of Milo. I took his cock in my hand and rubbed the cum up and down his shaft. After opening my mouth, I sucked Milo inside of me to lick off every last drop of Verano's cum.

Milo stiffened, as if he didn't *want* to like this, as if he shouldn't like this.

But he did.

His balls twitched, his dick hardening even more as my warm mouth sucked on his huge cock. I bobbed my head up and down on him and came back up for air. "Trying to get every last drop inside me. Don't want any to go to waste."

Verano watched from the bed, his gaze on my tits as they bounced the harder I bobbed my head. I glanced up at Milo through watery eyes and took all of him inside me, swallowing over and over, my throat so tight around him that I couldn't breathe.

Finally, Milo couldn't hold back his grunts anymore. He threw his head back and came deep down my throat. I stayed there for another few moments, then pulled his cock out of my mouth and swallowed all his cum too.

Milo might've been the deadliest man in all of this city, but he wouldn't stop me from getting everything I wanted.

Part 2

My husband had stripped me naked and tied me to a bed while I slept. I pulled on the restraints and glared at him sitting across from me in a dirty plastic lawn chair. We weren't at home, but in a sleazy motel somewhere.

"Let me out!" I screamed. "What are you doing?"

With his sharp jaw clenched, he tilted his head to the side and glanced out the blinds. Without looking back at me, he stood up and walked to the door, his gun sticking out of the waistband of his suit.

"Milo!" I shouted. "Let me out of here! Where are you going?! I want–"

I smacked my lips closed when five of his trusted men walked into the motel room, including Verano. My mouth dried, and I scrambled to *attempt* to hide myself underneath the sheets. But the more I moved, the more attention I drew to myself.

Milo shut the door and turned to the group of gangsters. "Fuck her."

"What?" Verano asked, jaw slack.

"Fuck. My. Wife."

When Verano still didn't make a move toward me, Milo grabbed him by the collar and slammed him against the wall, his gun pressed against Verano's temple. "How do I make myself any fucking clearer?!"

After the other night, Milo must've threatened Verano with a punishment worse than anything that I could imagine. Especially if Verano didn't want to lay a single finger on me now that I was the one tied up.

The guards shuffled around as my husband released Verano and walked to the other side of the bed, waving his gun between the guards and me. "Don't make me wait. Every single one of you is going to fuck her."

"Milo!" I screamed. "You're not going to fucking do this!"

But when the first guard pulled off his belt and my husband smirked at me, I knew that he was serious. Milo was about to go as far as I had the other night, maybe even farther with how many men he brought here.

The first one shoved himself into me and filled me up, his balls smacking against my aching wet pussy with every thrust. I sucked in a breath and grasped onto the restraints, glaring at my husband as pleasure rushed through me. Once he came inside me, the second guard thrust himself into me. And then the third. And the fourth.

And then when I was dripping with cum from four different men, Verano lined his cock up at my entrance, seized my hips, and shoved his fat cock into my pussy. I clenched around him, not feeling much with the other men… but with him…

I arched my back and sank my head into the pillow. "God!"

"Is this what you fucking wanted?" Milo growled, inches from my face. "Does getting fucked by men who aren't your husband make you feel good? Does it make you feel pretty? Beautiful? Do I not do that enough?"

The entire time they had been pounding into me, he hadn't touched me once. But I wanted my husband's hands all over me, touching me while his men thrusted into me and used me like the dirty little whore that I was.

So I pressed my lips together and smirked at him as a response.

He harshly grabbed my chin. "Answer me!"

"Yes!" I growled. "They make me feel sexier than you ever have."

Which was a lie that he saw through, but still... It made him furious.

After turning the gun on me, he shoved it into my mouth and moved closer to me. "Don't be a fucking brat with me right now. I have the power, Lara, and you have none. You've never had any in this family, no matter how long you've been my wife."

When he pulled the gun from my mouth, he yanked off my restraints, grabbed my hair, and pulled me off the bed. Verano's cock fell out of my pussy as I collapsed onto the ground at my husband's feet.

"You're a bas–"

"Shut her the fuck up, Verano," Milo ordered.

Verano crawled off the bed and shoved his dick in my mouth.

"This is your fucking punishment," Milo snarled. "Don't you ever tie me up again."

I bit back the urge to taunt him, because I knew he could do so much worse. I had seen the things he had done to countless people who had betrayed him, the agony that he had caused, the torture and blood in our basement.

"Verano is my bitch," he said, lips millimeters from mine. "Not yours. He does what I say, what I ask, what I demand, and if he doesn't, I blow the head off his body while *I* fuck you. Understand?"

I pressed my lips together around Verano's cock and glared up at my husband through burning eyes filled with tears. Verano hit the back of my throat over and over, making me gag and spit up on his cock.

"Nod your fucking head," Milo growled, grabbing a fistful of my hair and slamming my head up and down on Verano's cock. "What do you say?"

"Fuck... you..." I said between thrusts.

He tugged my hair back harshly so I'd stare up at him and slapped me hard on the cheek. "Yes, boss. That's the only correct answer after you betray me, fuck one of my men in front of me, and have no sympathy for it."

Not husband. Boss.

After tightening, I dug my almond-shaped nails into Verano's thighs in an attempt to push him away so I could breathe. But I knew Milo would never *ever* allow it. He'd probably keep having his men fuck me even when I passed out from lack of oxygen, make me wake up to cock in all of my holes.

When Verano pulled out of me, I spit up at my husband. "Fuck. You."

"Ruin her," Milo growled, storming to the dirty white lawn chair and sitting, his dark gaze fixed on me and his gun sitting in his lap, over that huge bulge in the front of his suit pants. And I wouldn't doubt that he had already made a mess in his pants, watching me sleep with his most trusted men, attempting to hide it behind that scowl and his gun. My husband would reject that this ever made him feel good. But it did.

Man, it did.

mafia playboy

RACHEL'S skinny ass stood naked in front of one of my many penthouse windows when I opened my front door. She placed her hands on the glass and glanced back at me, trying to be sexy but just looking embarrassing as fuck.

"You're home so soon," she murmured, stalking toward me and swaying her hips from side to side. "I expected you to be out all night on family business. Your father told me that you had a job to take care of."

"What are you doing here?" I asked, closing my front door behind me and setting my gun on the counter.

After catching Charlene, the girl with the nerdy glasses and nervous smile who lived two floors down, in the elevator only a few moments ago and *fucking up* my entire conversation with her, I had officially had the worst damn night of my life.

All I wanted was to shove Charlene against those elevator doors, fuck her senseless, and kill anyone who tried to stop me. She had been giving me those dangerous, sultry eyes for too fucking long now. And I hadn't been able to do shit about it.

Now, I had to deal with this bitch.

Rachel undid the buttons on my shirt with her pink manicured fingers and pressed her fake tits against my chest. For her spending almost ten thousand dollars on them, they came out horrible.

"I wanted to see you," she murmured into my ear, gently laying a kiss on my neck.

"How'd you get into my house?"

She brushed her hand over the front of my suit pants, and I cursed underneath my breath. Not because I liked her or wanted her, but because I could do nothing but imagine her hands as Charlene's hands running all over my body.

"The key you gave me, silly."

But I never gave that bitch a key.

When she slipped her hand into my pants, I growled and grabbed her, shoving her toward the couch. She landed with a thud, a breathless expression on her face. "Turn over," I growled at her.

If I was going to fuck her to relieve my stress from the day, then I didn't want to see her face. Shit, since I met Charlene, I didn't want to see any other woman's face as I fucked them to get off. All I wanted was to picture me sliding into Charlene's tight little pussy, her moans drifting through the air, her body becoming tense as fuck in my hands.

Grunting, I stared up at the ceiling and gripped Rachel's ass as I pounded into her. Her ass was small as shit and didn't have any meat on it, nothing to grab, nothing like Charlene's. I moved my hands to her hips and pulled her toward me with every thrust.

She was so boney, so skinny. She was the kind of woman that my entire family went for, the type of whore that I used to love having in the bedroom. But now I couldn't get Charlene's body out of my fucking mind. From her wide hips, ass, tits, and thick as fuck thighs… god, she was fucking perfect.

I squeezed my eyes closed. "So fucking perfect."

Rachel giggled underneath me. "You like that, baby?"

Instead of answering her, I grunted and furrowed my brows. All I could do was imagine her naked on my bed, thrusting her against the ceiling to floor length windows and fucking that cute expression off her pretty face.

I wanted to make that innocent girl my little fucktoy. I wanted her mind numb as I fucked her raw. I wanted her to think of nobody else ever except me, about nothing else other than how good she felt while she was with me.

Her pussy tightened around my cock, squeezing every fucking inch of it. I had jerked off so many fucking times thinking about shoving my cock into her tight holes that I didn't want to wait until I could finally have her. I needed to be inside her tonight.

"Are you going to come for me?" Rachel asked, drawing me out of my daydream again.

Gripping her head, I shoved her face into the pillow so she couldn't speak anymore. She was nothing but a bitch, a nag, someone for me to use while I figured out how the fuck I would make Charlene mine.

"Shut the fuck up, Rachel."

She said something muffled into the pillow, moaning or some shit. And I went back to thinking about Charlene's pussy clamping down on my cock and milking out all the cum from my balls. I didn't even know the woman, but I wanted to get her pregnant. I wanted her belly full and round with my kids.

"Fuck, Charlene," I grunted, pulling out of Rachel and coming on her ass.

There was no way in hell that I'd come inside her ever again. Not since Charlie gave me that smile in the elevator the other night, behind those thick-as-fuck glasses that were almost too big for her face.

"Charlene?!" Rachel snapped, turning around completely naked in my bed, scowling at me, and smacking me hard on the cheek. "Who the fuck is Charlene?"

My eyes rolled back in my head as the orgasm continued to shoot through my body and the last bead of cum dribbled out of my cock and onto my mattress. I gave it one last, good stroke with my hand and grunted, closing my eyes and wanting nothing but to kick this bitch out. I had no use for her anymore.

"Charlene?! Who the fuck is she?!"

"She's none of your fucking business," I growled, pulling my suitpants back up my legs and zipping them up. I didn't want her or any of the family knowing about Charlie. She was mine and only mine, and I–the fucking playboy of the family–hadn't even scored a date with her yet.

"You just moaned out her name!" Rachel screamed, storming toward me and shoving her hands against my chest. "She means something to you. She's someone. Tell me who the fuck she is. I deserve to know."

"You deserve nothing!" I shouted. "You're nothing but a gold-digging whore."

She slapped me hard across the face again, and I had to do everything in my fucking power not to kill her right then and there. I should've fucking done it too, because I knew she'd do everything in her power to stop Charlie from giving me the time of fucking day.

Rachel was nothing but a problem that I didn't want.

When she went to slap me again, I grabbed her hand and shoved her hard toward the door to my penthouse. I refused to deal with her shit anymore. I didn't care what the rest of the family thought. I never wanted to be with someone like her.

"Get out of my fucking house," I shouted, throwing her out the door naked along with her clothes. "And don't come back. Don't contact me again. Don't even show your fucking face in any of my family's establishments, or I'll kill you myself."

Face red with anger, she gritted her teeth at me, pulled on her clothes, and stomped down the hallway toward the elevators. I slammed the door and walked back into my home, pulling out a bottle of whiskey and sipping it right from the glass.

Charlene would be mine tonight. I didn't care what it took.

mafia brothers

PART 1

Bound to the living room doorway, I stood spread eagle naked in the middle of the family home. My wrists were bound tightly to rope that hung from the top corners of the doorway, my ankles to the bottom corners, and my thighs to the center.

Compensation. Payment. Reparation.

That's what my step-dad told me all I was to him and his brothers after Mom–if I could even call her that anymore–screwed them over. Apparently she thought stealing half a million dollars from the three richest men in town would go over well for her. And it must've, because she was off the grid without a trace and I was stuck paying the consequences of her actions to the half-Italian, half-Greek assholes.

Cassius: The Ferrari Family's Lawyer

Constantine: The Ferrari Family's Doctor

Cesar: The Ferrari Family's Boss

Cassius, Constantine, and Cesar sat on the couches, smoking cigars and talking business. I wriggled helplessly as the vibrator fastened between my legs made me cry out in pleasure. "P-Please, make it s-stop."

I had been bound here for the past three hours with the toy

sending vibrations to my clit on a higher and higher setting each hour. Pleasure gathered between my thighs, and I moaned out as an orgasm ripped through my body.

Constantine placed his glass of sambuca down on the oak table and walked over to me, twirling his favorite toy–a knife–between his fingers. He stalked around me, the thud of his shoes echoing through the large room.

"Helpless little fucktoy," he murmured against the back of my neck, drawing the blade up my trembling inner thigh. He paused inches before my cunt and pressed the tip gently on my skin, nearly hard enough to pierce the flesh. "Poor thing."

"Let me out," I said between gritted teeth. "*You asshole.*"

Harshly seizing my throat, he pulled my body back toward him so I felt every single flexed muscle against my naked backside, even his throbbing bulge nestled between my ass cheeks. He drew his blade up even further, millimeters from the vibrator Cassius had stationed there earlier.

"You need to learn your fucking place," he growled.

"I'm sorry if I didn't make myself clear enough," I snapped back. *"Fuck. You."*

After ripping the vibrator away from my cunt, he grabbed a fistful of my hair and yanked it back roughly. He nestled his knife between the top of my pussy lips, pushing them apart, the blade against the soft flesh. "Each of us is going to fuck this tight hole, then you're going to clean us off with this bratty little mouth of yours," he said.

"Go to hell," I growled. "No way will I put you into my mouth."

"We'll see about that, you filthy fucking slut."

After slicing the ropes around my wrists with a knife, he bent me over at the waist and whipped out his huge dick while his brother's watched. My pussy throbbed. When he plunged into me, I cried out in pleasure.

Cesar chuckled from the table. "All that complaining and you still moan for him."

Cassius leaned back in his seat, his sharp jaw clenched and his hand on the thick bulge in his suit pants. I clenched around Constantine. Cassius wasn't much of a talker, but damn he was the dirtiest one of them all.

He had been the one to strip me naked and tie me up here against my will.

"All you have to do is submit, you pretty little slut," Constantine murmured into my ear.

"Never," I growled. "Especially not to–"

When he pressed his knife's sharp edge to my throat, I sucked in a sharp breath and stiffened. My pussy clamped down around him, the warmth growing inside me. Every thrust, he pushed me closer and closer to the edge–of the blade and of an orgasm.

"Lost for words?" he taunted.

"No, you bast–"

Before I could finish my sentence, he slipped the blade up to my lips and pressed the tip against my bottom. "Say it," he dared. "Finish your sentence and see what happens to your pretty face."

Pleasure shot through me, and I screamed out. Wave after wave of ecstasy crashed through my body, sending me over the edge for the umteenth time tonight. He thrust into me hard and fast one last time before grunting deeply into my ear and stilling.

"Fuck, your tight little cunt loves milking out that cum," he groaned, slowly pulling out.

After putting out their cigars, Cesar and Cassius walked over to us. Cassius took my hips in his large hands next, pulling them back and forcing me to bend over. Constantine walked around to my front and grabbed a fistful of my hair.

"Open your fucking mouth," he growled, shoving his cock against my lips.

I snapped my mouth shut.

"Come on, you dirty slut," he said. "I know you want to taste yourself."

The longer I refused to obey, the harder and harder he pressed his dick to my lips. And when he had had enough, he pinched my nose closed to stop me from breathing any air. I struggled against him, desperately trying to push him away to breathe.

Cassius thrust into me from behind, and I swallowed a moan, my throat squeaking. He seized my wrists in one hand and pulled them behind my back, letting my tits hang. Reaching around my torso, he took one in his hand, groping the flesh and tugging harshly on my nipple.

"Open your mouth," Constantine ordered.

"Mmnpft. Mmnpft."

"You're being a bratty little bitch today," he warned. "As soon as you open this mouth–*and you will*–I'm going to ruin it. Tomorrow morning, your useless throat will be sore from how hard I'm about to fuck it."

I tried to hold my breath for as long as I could, my pussy wrapped tightly around his brother's cock. And when I couldn't take it any longer, my body forced me to open my mouth to breathe. But as soon as my lips parted, Constantine's cock was in my mouth and down my throat, pounding against the back of it.

I gagged on his dick, eyes widening. He released my nose and gripped my hair with both hands. "There we fucking go, you fucking slut," he growled, yanking me forward by the hair every time he thrust into me. "Take that big dick down your throat and taste yourself."

Both brothers pounded into each of my holes, spitroasting me until I could barely take it anymore. Spit and drool covered my chin, dripping onto the floors in the Ferrari's family home. Cassius's thrusts were harder and deeper than his brother's, reaching my cervix *every single time.* I gripped onto his hand, slicing my nails into his wrist and moaning.

"Gargle it," Constantine said. "I want that throat talking to me."

I parted my lips slightly, coughing up spit while he hit the back of my throat over and over again. He placed the tip of his knife underneath my chin and forced me to look up at him through teary eyes as my throat squeaked.

"You're so fucking pretty filled with dick."

A wave of heat rushed through me again, and I clamped down on Cassius who grunted. The sound of his moan sent me over the edge, and I sucked harder on Constantine, getting off every last drop of my juices.

After Cassius pulled out of me, he walked over to my front as Cesar took his place behind me. From my side, Constantine pulled out of me, grabbed a fistful of my hair in one hand and chin in the other, then pulled them apart so his brother could slip himself inside me before I had the chance to close it and put up another fight, because *God* did I want to.

Cassius took my chin in his hand as I sucked on his dick. "Good girl," he whispered.

My entire body shook in pleasure, loving the way he praised me.

I opened my mouth wider, eager to please him without the intentions of being a brat, and flicked my tongue against his balls. He grunted and gripped his dick and balls in his large, scarred hand, shoving them into my mouth too.

"Look at the good little slut," Cesar groaned behind me, pounding away. "So desperate for her step-uncle's fucking cum, she's sucking his balls too. Get them all fucking wet, so he can drag them across your face and make you even prettier."

After I sucked hard on them, Cassius pulled his dick and balls out of my mouth and dragged them all over my face, ruining my makeup even more and decorating my cheeks with strings of spit. Then he placed the head of his cock at my lips again.

"Am I prettier for you?" I asked him, desperate to hear his praise.

"So fucking pretty," he cooed, sliding himself back inside me and using me to get off. "Even prettier with cock in your tight, warm mouth."

Cesar held onto my wrists from behind, pulling them toward him with every quick thrust to sink himself deeper and deeper into my pussy. "Fuck," he grunted, mumbling something in Italian. "Your pussy is so much better than your mother's. Tighter." *Grunt.* "Wetter." *Grunt.* "Easier to fill."

Cassius and Cesar came almost at the same time, both slamming into me. I choked on Cassius's cum as it shot down my throat. And when they both pulled out of me, Cesar's cum dripped down my inner thighs. They had filled up my tight holes with so much cum that I couldn't even hold it all inside myself anymore.

"Suck all that cum off my cock," Cesar said, when I took him into my mouth. "Clean off your daddy's dick." He laced a hand into my hair and bobbed my head back and forth. "Rub that swollen clit for daddy. I want you to think about *me*, about what your mother has done to *me*, about why your slutty mouth is making up for it."

I rubbed my clit in small circles, bringing myself to the edge.

So close.

So freaking close.

"Stop," he growled, pulling out of my mouth once I had cleaned him off. His cock smacked against his thigh with a thud, then he grabbed a fistful of my hair and pulled me back to a standing position. "Redo her binds, Cassius. This little whore isn't finished for tonight."

Part 2

One Week Before the Night

After Cesar, that annoying bastard of a stepfather, passed out in his bedroom, Mother snuck down the hallway in the middle of the night. I sat in the dark living room near the ceiling-to-floor windows, impatiently waiting for her to leave like she usually did at this time.

She always slipped out at four in the morning to see her fling, once Cesar returned from working all night at the *club*. Who would've thought that this bitch wanted a fling after her own husband had millions of dollars and would kill anyone and everyone for his family?

Me.

I ripped a piece of skin from my inner cheek with my teeth. I had predicted this from the moment Mother introduced me to Cesar. That witch couldn't keep a relationship, but she didn't know what she had gotten herself into this time.

Because Cesar Ferrari would kill anyone. For any reason.

After she strapped on a pair of red-bottoms in the foyer, she slipped out the door and shut it quietly behind her. I waited a few more moments to make sure she was really gone, then hopped off the couch and walked toward the master bedroom.

Cesar had pissed me off earlier, completely embarrassing me in front of his brothers.

And payback was a fucking bitch.

Once I cracked the door open a couple inches, I peered into the room to ensure that Cesar really was sleeping. He laid on his stomach, the moonlight bouncing off his muscular bare back. I clenched and pushed the door open enough to slip into the room.

While Mother had never raised me to be a whore, I was learning from her example. Getting what I wanted from sleeping with men who had money, who had power, and who had prestige. Except I didn't need any of that.

All I needed was for Cesar Ferrari to hurt for ruining my life.

Once I tiptoed to Mother's side of the bed, I sat on the edge, lifted the blankets, and curled up on the mattress with my back facing toward him. I inched my ass backward, pressing it against his side, my pussy throbbing underneath my silky robe.

"Come here," he murmured into my ear, slinging his arm over my waist and pulling me closer until his cock nestled against my ass. My nipples hardened. I tugged on them and let out a low moan, gently bucking my hips back and forth across his hardening dick.

I might've been with his brothers earlier, but I had never once slept with my stepdad. I had prided myself on that fact for so damn long. Yet tonight it didn't matter. I would hurt him the way he had hurt me.

Fuck him.

Literally.

A low grunt escaped his full lips, and he dropped one of his hands to between my thighs and cupped my mound. I squeezed my legs together, the heat building between them and bit my lip to hold back another soft moan.

"Let me hear those moans, baby," he mumbled against my neck, his stubble tickling me.

He shoved two fingers between my pussy lips and then right into my tight hole. I threw my head back and placed a hand over my mouth, the pressure building higher and higher in my core. He felt huge against my ass.

He mumbled something in Italian. "You're soaked, Meredith."

Thank fuck I looked like Mother from the back.

I grinded myself against his cock and clenched. With his fingers still sliding in and out of me, he rubbed my clit around in torturous circles with his thumb, his hot breath fanning my neck and making me even tighter. "You're never this wet."

Well, tonight I was.

Maybe it was a mix between how much I wanted my revenge, how Cesar had been looking at me lately, and how much both his brothers had come in my pussy earlier during that yacht party.

As his fingers dipped deep inside me, all I could hear were my choppy breaths and the wet sounds my pussy was making for him echoing throughout the room. I spread my legs wider to give him better access, the pressure building up inside me even quicker than it had while I was with his brothers.

A guttural growl escaped his throat, and he wrapped his muscular arm underneath my top leg to spread my thighs even further apart. I whimpered when he pressed his hard cock against my entrance and screamed when he began pushing it inside me.

"Damn, you're pussy's tighter than usual for me," he murmured into my ear.

My pussy wrapped around his cock, and I clenched on him each time he pumped into me. He reached around my leg and groped one of my breasts, squeezing harshly. I grasped the bedsheets as tightly as I could, my nipple gliding against his rough palm.

Holy fuuuuck.

How could my whore of a mother have anything better than this? Why had she been sneaking out late at night to see another man when her own husband had nearly already made me come just by pushing himself into me?

He pounded inside of me. I bit my lip to muffle my moans as my legs began trembling. When he tugged on my nipples harshly, I arched my back. I threw my head into the pillow and moaned, legs trembling and mind numb as wave after wave of pleasure exploded through my core. Yet he didn't stop.

Instead, he gripped my hips with both his hands tightly and turned me onto my stomach. While I expected him to crawl between my legs, he straddled my hips and pushed his cock between my ass cheeks.

"Fuck, Meri," he grunted, wrapping his arms underneath mine and grasping my shoulders. He slammed himself into me, cursing in Italian and sucking on the crook of my neck. "So tight. So tight. So"–*thrust*–"fucking"–*thrust*–"tight."

I reached behind myself and spread my thighs apart with my hands to give him better–*deeper*–access. He growled into my ear and pounded into me harder, as if me spreading my thighs for him made him even more desperate.

"I don't care what you say this time, Meredith," he murmured against my throat. "I'm coming inside you and filling up this tight, wet hole with my cum tonight. Your pussy is begging for it."

I clenched, making him thrust so deep that he hit my cervix.

He didn't pull out, but continued to drive his hips even deeper against mine. "That desperate little whore in you wants it too." He grunted after a few more moments. "Milked the cum right out of my balls tonight, baby."

My lips curled into a smirk, and I pulled the blankets over my shoulders once he rolled off me. The room was dark, but I still didn't want to chance it. Because once he fell asleep, I'd slip out of the room and relish in my revenge.

———

The next morning, Cesar padded out into the living room.

"How'd you sleep last night?" I asked from the couch with a tea mug.

Without responding, he peered over at me, his gaze dropping to my nipples pressed against my white tank top for a brief moment, then to the hickey on my neck. Then he grabbed a coffee mug from Lily, his housekeeper. "Where's your mother?"

So grumpy.

"Don't know. Don't care," I said, sipping on my tea. "She's been gone all night."

"When did she leave?"

"After you fell asleep."

Tensing, he glanced over at me. I smiled sweetly at him and looped my finger around the strap of my tank top, moving it down toward my cleavage. Ever since Mother married him, we had both hated each other. And after he had plunged himself inside me last night, I still loathed him with my entire heart.

He and his brothers could fall off a cliff for all I cared.

Once I leapt up from the couch, I grabbed my purse on the counter and headed for the door. "Payback's a bitch." I stopped behind him and smirked, my lips inches from his ear. "Apparently one with a wetter and tighter pussy than my mother."

mafia maid

RICCARDO BIANCHI SCROLLED through his phone at the head of the dining table with an empty glass of whiskey in front of him. After wiping down the kitchen counter, I refilled the glass, my hand trembling from the nerves zipping through me right now.

I had worked for the Bianchi Family for nearly thirty years and had never asked for a night off because I had never quite needed it before now. Riccardo gave me more than enough time during the week to spend my days doing whatever I wanted with his dirty money.

But I wanted to go out Friday night with a man I had met at the grocery store. He had worked there for the past five years, but I had never gotten the courage to talk to him besides some desperate little smiles here and there.

"What's wrong?" Riccardo asked.

"N-Nothing!" I said too quickly

He grabbed my shaky hand, stopping me from pouring any more. "Ophelia."

Sucking in a breath, I placed the bottle of alcohol down on the counter and hurried toward the front of the table to distance myself. My hands shook so much that I clasped them together behind my back so he wouldn't see.

"Can I get Friday night off this week?" I whispered.

"You need to speak louder than that, Miss Daft," he said, returning to his phone.

"Can I get Friday night off this week?" I repeated.

"Why?"

I rocked back on my heels and chewed on my inner cheek. "For a date."

He snapped his gaze up to mine, his eyes darkening. "A date? With who?"

"His name is Jeff."

"Last name?"

"Holmes," I said, nerves building up inside me. "He works at the grocery store on Fifth."

"You've spoken with this man before?" he asked, tightening his hand around his glass.

"Yes."

"For how long?"

"Uhm," I said, my voice quieter. "A bit."

He returned to his whiskey and drank it down in one gulp. "No."

My eyes widened. "But–"

"I have a date Friday night and need you to cook," he said.

My stomach fell, and I turned around to head for the counter. "Oh," I said, trying not to sound too disappointed as I grabbed the rag to busy myself in cleaning the mess I had made in the kitchen tonight. "With who? The woman from the other night?"

"No," he said, voice heavy. "Someone else."

———

As a bead of sweat rolled down my forehead, I wiped it with the back of my hand and hurried around the kitchen to prepare Riccardo's meal with his date. He never brought many women back to his home, especially not on a first date, so she must've been important to him.

"Will she be here soon?" I asked as he walked out of the hallway dressed in the same clothes he had gone to work at Syndicate today, which meant that maybe… maybe she was someone close to him.

I mean, if he wasn't dressing up super fancy…

"She will," he said, sitting down at the dining table, not at the seat that I had set for them but one that faced the kitchen where I pulled two steaks off the skillet. He peered down at his phone to text her.

Fifteen minutes later, after rushing around the kitchen like a madwoman to make sure everything was perfect, I cleared my throat. "Riccardo, should I put the steak in the oven to keep it warm? Or will she be here soon?"

I glanced at the clock, realizing that I probably should've started cooking when she arrived and not any sooner. But I hadn't wanted to piss him off more than I had the other night when I asked for today off.

"Ah," he hummed, placing down his phone. "Turns out that she got held up in traffic." He stood up and walked to the opposite side of the table, pulling out the chair. "Why don't we eat together? Since she's not coming."

"Me?" I asked, eyes widening.

"Sit."

I swallowed hard and set one plate in front of him. "Mr. Bianchi, I–"

"Formalities now, Miss Daft?" he asked, his full lips curled into a smirk. "Sit down."

Hesitantly, I sat across from him with the meal that was supposed to be his date's.

We sat in silence for most of dinner, besides him asking me questions every now and then. Besides at some family holidays, I had never sat and had dinner with him. I had worked for him and his family for so long that it felt wrong.

But the longer the night went on, the more I relaxed. I even took a couple sips of the wine he had poured for me while he sipped on his third or fourth glass of whiskey for the night. If he wasn't careful he–

"You've known me for thirty years," he murmured, sipping his drink until his eyes turned glossy the way they did when he had a bit too much. "Do you think that I'm a bad man, Ophelia?"

"Of course not."

"Not even for making up an excuse that I had a date tonight, so you'd stay home?"

My eyes widened. "What?"

He stared at me, unapologetically.

"Why would you do that?" I whispered, heart pounding.

"Why would I do that?" he repeated, a dark and sinister tinge in his voice. "Because I've been desperate for you to notice me for the past thirty fucking years, Ophelia. And then you ask to leave me for another man during the time I'm scheduled to see you."

Heat gathered in my core, my breath catching in my throat. "W-What do you mean?"

Between his looks and his money, Riccardo Bainchi could have anybody on this planet. He had gone out with plenty of women who were half his age without wrinkles and stretch marks, those who could still give him kids.

I had dedicated my life to him, had given up all hopes and dreams I had because the money was nice and he treated me better than some of the other jobs I had in my teens. I never got a college education so the opportunities had always been limited. I had nothing to offer him.

Before I could voice any of those concerns, he was at my side. He took my chin in his hand, pulled me closer to him, and kissed me hard on the mouth. I stiffened in his hold for a brief moment, wondering if this was all some sort of… joke.

But Riccardo didn't make jokes, especially not with me.

"Riccardo," I whispered between kisses. "Wh-What are you doing?"

He seized my waist and lifted me onto the table, almost immediately dropping to his knees between my thighs. I leaned my arms back on the table to steady myself, my breath quickening.

"Fuck," he growled, drawing his stubble up my inner thigh. "I'm starving for you."

When he slipped his fingers underneath my dress and looped them around my panties, heat exploded through my core. I tensed and stared down at him, knowing that this was wrong, that this was all the alcohol talking.

He didn't care about me. Nobody did.

"Mr. Bainchi," I whispered. "We should stop."

After lifting and spreading my legs, he placed one of them on his shoulder and moved his lips closer to my cunt. He stared up at me through those dark eyes, daring me to say it again. "Tell me to stop, and I'll stop."

I stared down at him, brows furrowed together.

I didn't know what to do. I really didn't want him to stop. I hadn't been touched by someone like this in a very, very, very long time. I feared that I wouldn't be enough, that he would realize that he didn't really want this and would fire me for allowing this to happen.

"Say it," Riccardo growled.

Fuck.

"Say it, Ophelia," he ordered. "Or I won't stop until my cum is buried inside you."

"M-Mr. Bainchi," I whispered, nipples taut. "You're going to… to regret this, if you don't–"

Before I could finish my sentence, his mouth was on my pussy. He dragged his tongue across my clit, flicking the sensitive bead over and over. I jerked my knees up, the pleasure building faster than it ever had.

I thrust a hand into his hair, my legs trembling. "Mr. Bainch–"

With his mouth still on my cunt, he wrapped a hand around my throat and stared up at me through those dark eyes. "I've done a lot of fucked up shit in my life that I wish I could do over, but I would never regret this, Ophie."

Ophie?

My heart raced. He had only used that pet name for me after a long night, when all he wanted to do was forget about the world and relax in his home or when he had gotten a little too drunk and forgot that I was only his maid.

"Riccardo," I whimpered.

He plunged two large fingers into me. "This pussy is mine."

Entire body tensing, I nodded. "Y-Yours."

When he curled his fingers against my g-spot, I lost it and cried out in pleasure. My legs jerked uncontrollably underneath me, but he held them in place and continued massaging inside me, his eyes never leaving mine once.

"Good girl," he murmured to me.

"Riccar–"

He pulled his fingers out of me and sucked them into his mouth to clean them, and then he stood up, his cock hard against his suit pants. I inhaled sharply and stared down at how big he truly was, my heart racing.

After he slowly unbuckled his belt and pulled down his zipper, his cock sprung out and pressed against my entrance. I licked my lips and lifted my gaze to him, watching a wad of spit drip from his mouth and onto the head of his cock.

"Beg for it," he murmured. "Beg for me to fuck you like I've imagined all these years."

"Please," I whispered, nipples aching. "Please, fuck me. Pl–"

Before I could finish my sentence, he slammed himself into me. When I threw my head back to moan in pleasure, he buried his face into the crook of my neck and peppered kisses up and down the column of my throat to my lips.

Heat exploded through my core, and I moaned into his mouth. He pumped into me slowly at first, then with every passing moment, his thrusts became harder, faster, and rougher. I clutched onto his muscular shoulders, digging my nails into his flesh.

"M-More!" I cried out. "Harder, please, Riccardo!"

He rammed himself into me at a quickened pace, seized a fistful of my hair, yanked it back, and kissed me hard again. I slipped my tongue into his mouth, knowing that this was wrong, that he was my boss.

But I couldn't care anymore.

I had had a crush on him for decades now. I didn't want him to stop. I was so close to coming again and again and again for him. I wanted his cum inside me, wanted him to feel good *because* of me.

"Please, come inside me!" I cried.

A feral grunt escaped his mouth, and he plunged himself as deep as he could get, then stilled. I clutched onto his shoulders tightly and moaned out in pleasure as another orgasm ripped through my entire body.

"You're mine now, Ophelia," he growled into my mouth. "All mine."

mafia affair

"SWEETHEART," Cole, my husband, murmured as he walked into the house.

I glanced up from my laptop and chewed on the inside of my cheek. "It didn't go well today?" I asked, nervous for his response. He had been pitching his business idea to investors for the past three weeks, and this was his last hope.

"It went well," he said, loosening his tie and avoiding eye contact with me. He placed his keys on the kitchen table and sucked in a deep breath. "We raised one point five million dollars for this round by one investor."

Leaping up from my seat, I threw my arms around his shoulders and squealed. "Cole! Weren't you only asking for 800k? God, I knew that all you needed was one more investor to talk to. I'm so excited. This is amazing!"

"You think so?"

"Yes! We have to celebrate."

He relaxed in my embrace, wrapping his arms around my waist. I sighed softly and thanked whoever the hell was looking down on me that I had made the right decision, staying with Cole.

After those nights in New York City…

I had second thoughts.

I had worries and doubts.

I thought I had feelings for someone else.

And while I hadn't acted on them, sometimes Giovanni still drifted through my thoughts. But this feeling right here, holding my husband, seeing his happiness that his dreams were finally coming true, it was my everything.

"I already booked a room for us down at Rosebay," he said.

"Rosebay?" I repeated, eyes widening slightly. That was expensive.

He smiled and picked me up. "I thought it would... be a nice change for us."

"Go put this on," Cole said, handing me a new piece of lingerie once we settled into our room for the night. We had eaten a steak dinner and taken a walk down by the river together, and I couldn't have been happier.

We hadn't done that in years.

Years.

I curled my fingers around the silky chemises. "This?"

"Yes," he said, turning toward the dresser to pull off his tie.

"I thought you like it when I wear skimpy little lacy lingerie that barely covers anything."

I mean I wasn't complaining because I liked these more, but tonight was for him.

"Please," he said. "I want to see you wear it."

After nodding, I slipped into the bathroom to change. When I finished, my husband leaned against the opposite wall with his tie from earlier draped across his palm. "Come here," he murmured, beckoning me forward. He fastened it around my eyes, then led me to the bed.

I giggled anxiously. "Cole, we never do stuff like this."

"I thought we would spice it up tonight," he said, once I sat back on the bed. "Lie back."

Moving up the mattress, I laid on my back and hoped that I'd get wet for him tonight. How embarrassing would it be to be dry as hell after he had the biggest success of his life? What kind of wife would I be?

"Just like that," he murmured, fumbling around on the bed. "Shit."

"What?"

"I f-forgot something. I'll be right back."

He shuffled off the bed, and I listened to his footsteps lead into the next room. I took a deep breath, squeezing my eyes closed even though I couldn't see anything through the blindfold. And as I laid on the bed nearly naked, Giovanni drifted into my mind for a moment.

That night when he invited me onto his family's yacht for a party–as platonic friends–and I didn't have a bikini, so I wore nothing but my underwear and bra. I had almost betrayed my husband that night, but I resisted.

I pushed my thighs together.

Though I was so close. So close to chancing it all.

More guilt rushed through me. *No, Remi. Tonight is about my dear husband.*

The bed dipped beside me, and I sucked in a quick breath. I was so preoccupied with thoughts of that vile man that I hadn't even heard Cole approach. Before crawling onto the bed beside me, he placed his lips on my bare collarbone.

Heat gushed between my thighs, a small moan escaping my lips.

He peppered kisses down my chest and across the hem of my baby blue chemise, then dipped a hand between my thighs, sprawling it across my cunt. My legs fell outward, my heart pounding inside my chest.

"Cole," I whispered. "You never touch me like this."

No response.

After rubbing my aching cunt, he sucked on one of my nipples through the silky material making it hard. I arched my back and pressed my body against his, desperately wanting any friction that I could get. He hadn't touched me in weeks. Pitching his ideas had stressed him out big time lately.

"Please," I murmured. "More."

When he crawled between my legs, he drew his rough fingers up my inner thighs, pulled apart my legs, and spit right down on my pussy. I lifted my hips and pushed them toward him, desperate for him to be inside me already.

I squeezed my eyes closed underneath the blindfold and whimpered. "Please."

He pushed the head of his cock between my pussy lips and rubbed it across my clit, over and over in small torturous circles. I reached down and grabbed his thick cock from him, stroking it right up against my entrance.

"Please, fuck me," I cried. "I can't handle it anymore."

When he finally plunged himself inside me, I cried out in pleasure. Fuck, I didn't know what it was, but Cole felt huge. My walls were stretching, my cunt tightening around him. I reached for my blindfold, but he wrapped one of his large and rough hands around both of my wrists and pinned them to the bed above my head.

"Cole," I whispered. "You're so big."

Again, no response except a groan.

But my husband didn't grunt, growl, or groan in pleasure like this man did.

And this didn't feel like my husband. My husband's hands were smaller, less rough.

The only man's hands that I have felt like this before were…

"Your mind," I whispered, the start of an inside joke between me and Giovanni.

"Is twisted."

"Fuck," I whispered, heat exploding through my pussy.

"Fuck," he growled, pounding into me harder. "You just got so wet." Thrust. "Tight."

A moan–*a scream*–left my mouth, and I grasped the pillow tightly in my fists. My body trembled in his grasp, in his control as I desperately bounced my body back and forth to meet his thrusts. I needed more of this, more of him.

"More. More. More."

"A desperate little whore," he murmured, resting his forearms on either side of my head, his mouth against my ear and his warm breath on my neck. "I knew you'd turn into a fucking puddle for me."

I whimpered again.

"How long have you been wanting this?" he asked.

No response.

"How fucking long, Remi?" he growled.

Pressure rose in my core. I couldn't do that to my husband. I couldn't say it out loud. But another man was inside me right now. One that... One that Cole *had* to have let use me for some ungodly reason or another.

Unless Giovanni had done something to him.

"Don't make me ask again," he snarled.

"Since I met you," I said, the words tumbling out of my mouth before I could stop them.

He slammed into me harder and faster, pushing me over the edge. I arched my back and screamed out in pleasure, desperate for him to be flush against my body, for him to still inside me even when he–

"Fuuuuck," he growled, deep inside my pussy.

Another rush of pleasure shot through my body, and I cried out. *Fuck!*

After the high, I blew out a low breath. "My husband–"

"Tonight isn't about your husband," he growled. "It's about *me*."

"But he–"

"He got what he wanted, and I now have what I've wanted. *What I paid for.*"

"You're an investor?" I asked in a breathy whisper.

"An investor?" Giovanni chuckled. "Not for shitty ideas like his.

But for you." He ripped the blindfold off me, his dark eyes glinting in the moonlight. "I would do anything to be with you. And, God Remi, I mean *anything*."

mafia scandal

"YOU'RE FUCKING CHEATING ON ME?!" I growled after hurling our side table across the room.

Upon collision, it smashed to pieces and fell into a wooden pile in the middle of the kitchen floor. Annalise shrieked and leapt back, horror written across her face. "Dante! You're acting crazy. Stop it!"

"How the fuck am I supposed to act?!" I snarled. "My wife is cheating on me."

"I-I-I am not," she cried out.

But I had found the pictures that she had sent him and all the dirty late night texts. We had been married for less than a fucking year, and this was how she treated me? This was what she did when I murdered men in their homes for betraying our family.

What the fuck did she think would happen when I found out?

"Call him," I gritted out between my teeth. "Call him right fucking now."

"Dante," she whispered. "Y-You don't understand."

"You're fucking right, Anna. I don't understand." I balled my hands into tight fists, wanting to hurl them right into the walls. But if I split my knuckles open now, I wouldn't be able to kick this fucker's face in later. So I stepped toward her, snatched her throat, and pinned her against the wall. "I give you the fucking world, and you let another man slide his dick into you."

"N-No," she whispered. "I-I don't."

I snatched her phone from her, tapped on Rory's name in her contacts, and pressed *Call*. "Tell him to come over right now, and don't you fucking cry to him. I don't want him knowing that I'm about to kill his fucking ass until it happens."

"Rory," she whispered into the phone, tears streaming down her cheeks. "Come over."

While I couldn't hear what that dickhead sounded like, I would know what the insides of his stomach felt like tonight when I ripped it out as my lovely cheating wife watched. I didn't care how loudly she screamed at me to stop either.

———

Fifteen minutes later, Rory the Fuckhead knocked on the front door.

In a blind rage, I flung it open and seized him by her–

My hand wrapped around a woman's throat, and she yelped out and grabbed my arm, her huge eyes wide. She glanced past me at Annalise, her full lips parting and a soft, "Y-You're hurting me," escaping her mouth.

I released my hold and glared down at her. "Where the fuck is Rory?"

After she grasped onto the wall to catch her breath, she stared up at me through wide eyes. "What are you talking about?" She glanced past me at my wife again. "What's going on? I'm Rory."

"You're Rory?"

"I told you that it wasn't a man," Annalise whispered behind me.

"You're cheating on me with a woman?" I growled.

"Cheating?" Rory said, confusion crossing her face. "She said you were okay with it."

I snapped my gaze to my wife. "You did?"

"Come on, Dante," my wife whispered, walking past me to Rory.

She wrapped her arms around her waist from behind, her hands traveling to her full breasts, gently squeezing them. "Isn't she pretty?"

"Anna," I said, my dick twitching inside my suit pants.

"Let's face it," Annalise murmured, fingers curling over the hem of her shirt, tugging down on it in the middle of the hallway and exposing more of her tits. "We both knew that we would never settle down. Even with this ring on my finger."

"Anna," I warned, harsher this time.

"I see the way you look at other women at the club," she murmured. "Share her with me."

She dropped her mouth to the nape of Rory's neck, slowly dragging her full lips up the column of her throat and to her cheek, then gently kissed her. I glared at my wife, watching her touch another woman, my dick hardening.

"Anna," Rory whispered, staring up at me through innocent eyes. "Are you sure–"

From behind, Anna gently took Rory's chin and tilted it into her direction, so she could kiss her right on the mouth. Anna glanced at me for a moment as she slipped her tongue into Rory's mouth, turning Rory around and pressing her tits against hers.

Fuck.

"Anna," Rory murmured again between kisses, glancing nervously over at me.

My wife ran her hand down Rory's body, dragging her fingertips across her curves, then she brushed them against the front of Rory's skirt. She smirked against Rory's lips and moved her hand under the material.

"Come on, Dante," Anna taunted, moving her hand back and forth. "Touch her."

I drew my tongue across the back of my teeth and pressed a hand against the front of my pants, my balls warm and heavy. Anna pulled her wet fingers from Rory's skirt and stuck them into my mouth.

"She's so wet for you," my wife murmured.

When she pulled her fingers away from my mouth, I seized her wrist and continued sucking the juices off them. Rory inhaled sharply, eyes wide and nipples poking against her thin shirt.

Anna would drive me fucking mad one of these days.

With her free hand, Anna gripped my cock through my pants and slowly stroked it through the material. I groaned and tugged them both into the skyrise, slamming the door behind us and whipping off my belt.

"You and your little toy are going to pay for this, Anna," I warned.

"I highly doubt–" her bratty little mouth started to say.

Seizing her by the throat, I pinned her against the door and shoved her to the ground. "Open your mouth like a good girl, so I can fuck the brattiness right out of it," I growled. And when my wife wouldn't, I turned toward Rory. "Open her mouth."

Rory widened her eyes, but then dropped to her knees behind my wife. She tilted Anna's head back and kissed her from above, slipping her fingers into the corners of her mouth like fishhooks and pulled away, so my wife's mouth was wide open.

I laced my hand into her messy hair and slammed my dick into her throat. She gagged on my cock and went to jerk her head back, but Rory held her in place. I pulled my dick out of my wife and grabbed Rory's chin with my free hand, pulling her face over Anna's shoulder.

"Open," I ordered.

After Rory opened her mouth, I thrust myself into her throat. She stared up at me through wide, teary eyes, but didn't gag when I hit the back of it. I grunted and slammed my dick harder into her mouth, wanting to see how much and how hard she could take it. What would make her gag, drool, and jerk back on me?

But the harder I thrusted, the more she took.

"Fuck," I groaned.

"I knew you'd like that," Anna murmured. "She doesn't have a gag reflex."

Once I pounded my cock into her a couple more times, I

switched back to my wife, using both of their warm, wet mouths for my pleasure. It was the least Annalise could offer me after cheating for God knew how long with Rory.

"Get on the couch," I growled, finally pulling out of Anna's mouth. "Lie on each other."

Anna grabbed Rory's hand and skipped over to the couch, shedding her clothes. Once Anna sat down, she tugged off Rory's shirt, latched her mouth over one of Rory's nipples, and pulled her on top of her. Rory gasped, her tits swaying against my wife's chest.

I grunted again, positioned myself between their legs, and seized a fistful of Rory's hair. When I tugged back on it, I slammed myself into her tight little hole. She clenched around me and moaned as my wife sucked on her tits.

After curling my arm around her waist, I slid my fingers to her clit and rubbed small circles around the swollen bundle of nerves. She moaned again, this time into my wife's mouth, and pushed her hips back against mine. I thrust into her hard and fast, groping her ass with my free hand and staring down at my wife enjoying her toy.

"Lie back on the couch, Rory," I growled, pulling out. "My wife is going to eat you out."

Rory sucked in a sharp breath as they changed positions, with Rory on the couch and my wife on her knees between Rory's legs. Anna stuck her ass up in the air as she bent over and ate Rory's pussy.

I placed my hand on her lower back to arch it even harder, then I plunged into my wife's hole, grunting from how warm and tight she was. One hand in her hair, I shoved Anna's face against Rory's cunt.

"You want to cheat on me with a woman?" I snarled. "Suffocate in her fucking cunt."

Anna clenched around me, her tongue moving quickly against Rory's clit. I pounded harder into my wife, my balls heavy and aching to release inside her, to destroy her pretty pussy and fill it with my cum.

Rory jerked back, her eyes rolling and her head lolling. "F-F-Fuck!"

And when I heard Anna cry out in pleasure too, I slammed my hips against hers and stilled, dumping all my cum inside her tight pussy.

mafia boss

PART 1

"We shouldn't be doing this," I whispered to myself, hugging my arms around my body and rocking back and forth in the car. "We shouldn't be doing this. We shouldn't be doing this."

Ben slammed his foot on the car brakes, sending me flying forward, my seat belt digging into my throat. "Do you want to get out or not?"

My lips parted, fear running through every one of my veins. "We're too far deep, Ben. We could run for years, and he'd still find us." I glanced in the rearview mirror. "There's no running away from this."

"I'll take care of us," he said foolishly.

Didn't he know who our boss was? Didn't he know that Cristian Ricci didn't take any shit from anyone? How many times had that asshole tortured him? How many times had he continued to follow in his footsteps, and now, he wanted out?

"And how are you going to do that, Ben? Working odd jobs for the rest of our lives?"

When he pulled up to a stoplight, he reached in the backseat and grabbed one of the few duffel bags that I thought had his clothes inside and unzipped it. Cocaine … the bag was filled with at least $300,000 worth of drugs.

"You fucking stole from the mafia boss?!" My eyes widened, and I shook my head, staring back at the road in front of us.

This couldn't be happening. This couldn't fucking be happening. He was going to kill us.

"It'll be enough to hold us over until we can get out of the country." He grabbed my hand. "We can start a new life."

I yanked my hand away from him. I didn't want to start a new life with him. He had gotten me deep into this one … and I didn't want to leave it. The money, the power, and Cristian were enough to make me want to stay. But he was going to screw this all up for me.

After gazing into the backseat, my heart pounded in my chest. "How many fucking bags did you steal?"

Earlier, when he told me to get into the car, it was dark. I could barely see into the backseat, but now that I was actually looking … there was at least over a million dollars' worth.

"Relax."

"Stop the car," I said, my knee bouncing.

"I'm not stopping the car. Cristian will find us." He pulled off of the highway, heading onto the back roads and into the darkness of the woods.

A black SUV picked up speed behind us, on our fucking tail.

I leaned my head against the headrest, threw my hands over my face, and said, "They already have, you fucking idiot."

Ben hit the gas, speeding deeper into the forest. I stared straight ahead while he looked back at the SUV behind us.

"Ben!" I screamed, another SUV pulling right out into the road and stalling in the middle of our lane.

Ben hit the brakes, just enough to stop the car before we collided.

Four guards with guns hopped out of the SUV in front of us, and three hopped out of the one behind us. All their guns were trained on us. I felt like I was about to have a heart attack, my heart racing faster than it ever had before. I put my hands up into the air, tears streaming down my face.

Someone threw my door open and yanked me out. I fell onto my knees on the harsh cement, feeling the skin break. Their guns were trained on me as one picked me up by the arm, wrapped a blindfold around my eyes, and tied my hands behind my back.

"I fucking hate Ben," I whispered to myself. "I fucking hate him."

"Shut the fuck up." Someone pushed me into the backseat of one of the SUVs, and then the SUV did a U-turn and headed back in the direction of Cristian Ricci's home.

The whole time, my knees were bouncing, my heart was racing, and I wished that they had just killed me there.

I had never been punished by Cristian, but Ben had. And … I'd rather be dead than to be waterboarded, to have my nails pulled off, or to have his knife slide into my flesh.

After a thirty-minute drive, the SUV stopped. The guards pulled me out, dragging my feet on the gravel, and into a room. Unlike the mafia boss's home, the room was freezing and made all the little hairs on my arm stand up.

I didn't know how many men were here, but I could tell that there were many. At least seven of them, plus him. They pushed me onto my knees, and I tried to hold my tears in. Why was this happening? Why did I listen to Ben? We hadn't been together like that for almost a year now … yet I still foolishly trusted him.

Now, I would pay for it with my life.

Through my blindfold, I could see Ben's faint outline fall next to me. And I couldn't help the tears from racing down my cheeks. Cristian hadn't ever seen me cry before, and I had hoped that it stayed that way, but now that this was all ruined, I didn't care.

I listened to Cristian's footsteps, approaching me. He took a deep breath, and I pressed my lips together. What would he think of me after this? How would he kill me? Quickly, so I didn't feel pain? Or so slowly, so I paid for everything that Ben had done?

"Take them off," he said in his thick Italian accent.

Someone ripped off my blindfold, the bright lights blinding me. When my eyes finally adjusted, I gazed over at Cristian, who stood a few feet away with a gun in his hand. He stared at me with a clenched jaw and shook his head in disappointment. I gazed at the ground, unable to keep his intense stare. I felt like he saw right through me with it, like he knew every single one of my thoughts, could feel my pain … yet he didn't care.

"Stand," he said.

We stumbled to our feet, and I swallowed hard, unsure of what he would do next.

"Look at him, Principessa," Cristian demanded.

I swallowed hard, brows furrowed together, and glanced over at Ben, the man who made me betray the mafia boss, the man I once loved with all my heart, the man who got me into this mess.

"What do you see in him?"

My heart raced. What'd he want me to say? That I saw nothing? That I saw a weak man?

"Charm … love … adoration …" he said.

I gazed back at Cristian, begging with my teary eyes not to do this. "Please …"

He clutched the gun harder in his hand, his jaw tense. "Look at him and tell me what you fucking see."

Hesitantly, I gazed back at Ben. "I see the man I used to date … and … love."

"What else do you see?" he asked me.

Ben gazed at me, his lips quivering. Though I didn't like him like that anymore, we had spent so much time together, so many good memories of when we were younger.

"I see us riding the carousel horses on the boardwalk, running down the beach with the sand in our toes, lying under the stars and—"

He pulled the trigger, and a bullet went straight through Ben's head. My eyes widened, and I let out a piercing scream, backing away from him. Blood splattered everywhere, and Ben's body smacked hard against the ground while a puddle of thick red blood formed under him.

Cristian curled a hand around the back of my head, dragging me closer to Ben's body, and forced me to look at him. "What do you see now, Principessa?"

I parted my lips, tears streaming down my face. Oh my God … oh my God …

He was going to kill me like that too. He was going to leave me in a puddle of my own blood for nobody to ever find ever again.

He pushed me closer to him, his grip never loosening. "What do you fucking see?"

"I … I see … a dead man."

After chuckling menacingly, he pushed me away from him, tilted his head, and stared. I stumbled and grasped the sides of a table, holding myself up. My heart raced in my chest, and I didn't know what to think. I glanced around the room, seeing the seven other guards blocking all exits. There was nowhere to run, not that I'd be able to hide from him anyway.

"That will be you next if you don't answer every single one of my fucking questions." He stepped closer to me, and I stepped back. "Do you understand?"

I nodded. "Yes …"

"Why'd you follow Ben?"

"I didn't know that he was … he was running from you." I grasped a chair, pulling it in front of me.

He snatched it, threw it to the ground, and stepped toward me. "Wrong answer."

"I … I followed him because …" Why did I fucking follow him again? Because I was a dumb fucking woman. "Because I trusted him."

He stepped closer to me, grasped a fistful of my hair in one hand, and put the muzzle of his gun under my chin. "One last chance to answer me correctly, Principessa."

My fingers shook, and I stared right into his brown eyes. They were a wrathful kind of dark. A look full of sin and hurt and betrayal and intense anger.

I parted my lips and cursed myself for what I said next because even I didn't know if it was the truth or not. "Because I want out."

After pulling the gun away from me, he snatched my chin in his hand, pressing his fingers harshly into me. "You don't fucking get it, do you?" He pulled me closer, and I could feel the gun in his waistband. He glared down at me with so much rage. "You're mine, Principessa. I own you."

I nodded, hoping he'd give me some space … but I knew it wouldn't be that easy. He was going to give me hell for this, hell for trying to leave him, especially after everything that had happened between us.

"I can give you a world of so much fucking pain that you'll wish I'd killed you with that *stronzo*, or I can make you feel good, Principessa." He tilted his head down at me. "Do I make myself clear?"

I swallowed hard, my whole body tense, and nodded, not wanting to end up like Ben, who was dead on the floor.

He stepped back from me. "Good …" His gaze raked down my body. "Now, take off your clothes."

My eyes widened. "My clothes?"

"You didn't think you'd get out of this punishment-free, did you?"

He set the chair back on the ground a few feet away and sat down on it. "You're not going to make me say it again, are you?" He gazed over at Ben on the ground, then back at me, and grimaced, as if to say, *I could still kill you, if you'd like.* "Your choice."

I pressed my lips together, staring at all the guards in this room. Fuck this fucking guy. I tugged off my shirt and pulled down my pants, standing in just my bra and underwear in front of the mafia boss himself and several of his closest guards.

"Tick. Tock." He gazed into my eyes, waiting for me to continue.

Before I could let out a growl, I hesitantly unclipped my bra and let it slide down my arms, my breasts bouncing out of it. I watched the men gaze over and tried to ignore the heat pooling between my legs. I pushed down my panties and stepped out of them, covering my breasts with my arms.

"Arms down," he said, waving his gun.

I took a deep breath, my pussy clenching, and let my arms hang by my sides. He stared at my body for a long time, just taking in every inch, lingering on my tits and my throbbing pussy, then his lips curled into a smirk.

"Principessa, you're not ever going to do anything foolish like that again, are you?"

"No," I said, my voice cracking.

"No?"

"No, sir."

"And why's that?"

"Because …" I took a deep breath. "You own me."

"That's right," he said. "I choose who gets to put their cock all the way down that fragile throat of yours. I choose who gets to fuck your tight little ass." He gazed at his guards. "I can let them all fuck you right here while I watch, and you can't say anything about it. Do you understand?"

I pressed my lips together, my heart racing. When I didn't say anything, he cleared his throat and walked over to me, posturing over my naked body.

"Do. You. Understand?"

I nodded. "Yes, sir."

"Good." He paused for a long moment, stepped away from me again, eyes never leaving mine, then he tilted his head in the direction of one of his guards.

The guard walked over to me, and my eyes widened.

Oh my fucking God. This guy was absolutely psychotic. He wasn't fucking kidding.

I backed away, shaking my head, yet the heat in my core grew hotter. The guard, Marco, was one of Cristian's closest. He was big, brawny, and absolutely terrifying. I stared at Cristian as Marco tugged off his shirt, undid his belt, and pushed down his pants. Cristian's eyes were clouded with anger and rage.

"Anywhere but her pussy, Marco." He smirked at me. "Her pussy's mine."

Marco picked me up, sat on the table, then placed me right on top of him, my back against his chest. I pulled my legs together, trying to hide my pussy from all the other guards and from Cristian. I didn't want him to know that ... whatever he was planning ... wasn't a punishment for me.

Marco spread my legs, placing my feet on the opposite sides of his thighs so everyone could see my glistening pussy, and pressed himself against my ass. My pussy tightened, readying for the punishment I was about to get. He pushed himself inside of me, and I squirmed in his arms, my tits bouncing. He dug his fingers into my sides and held me in place. I gazed up at the bleak ceiling.

Fuck. Fuck. Fuck. Fuck. Fuck. He was so big—his arms, his body, his cock.

"Eyes on me, Principessa." I could hear the smirk in Cristian's voice. "I want to see that pretty face of yours before I let my men ruin it."

I gazed over at him, my brows furrowed. He stared at me like he owned me because he did and placed his hand on his thigh. I glanced down at his light-gray suit pants, seeing the imprint of his cock against it. God, I never thought this would be happening. I had dreamed of a moment with him for years now ...

"Spread her legs, Marco. I want to see how desperate her pussy is for a cock," he said.

Marco curled his arms under my legs and spread them wider, so everyone could see his cock ram into my ass. With every thrust, my tits bounced. Marco grasped one in his hand, tugging on my nipple. Cristian gazed at me, his jaw clenching slightly.

I tried to suppress my moans, but the pressure was too much. I opened my mouth to let out a small whimper but couldn't stop myself from screaming instead. Marco groaned under me, thrusting his cock harder into me. And I continued to moan, louder and louder each time. I'd been waiting so long for this.

Cristian nodded to another guard, who walked over to me, knelt on the table with us, pulled down his pants, and forced his cock down my throat. I gagged on it as he tangled his hand in my hair, face-fucking me.

I looked over at Cristian, like I knew he wanted me to, and moaned on the guard's cock, my pussy clenching over and over and over. God, I needed Cristian inside of me, thrusting his cock deep into my pussy, filling me up, taking me.

He stood up and nodded to one of his other guards, who walked over to me and pulled out his cock too.

"Why don't you take another one?" Cristian said, walking closer to me.

One of the men thrust into my mouth a few times, then the other, then back, over and over while he stalked toward me, drawing his fingers up the insides of my thighs and teasing me.

"Who's letting you feel good?" Cristian asked me.

I gagged on one of their cocks, spit drooling out of my mouth, and tried to answer. But when nothing coherent came out of my mouth, he slapped my pussy hard with his hand.

"Who's making you feel good?"

The guard pushed himself all the way down my throat, and Cristian wrapped his hand around my neck, squeezing tightly. My cheeks flushed, and I stared up at him with tears in my eyes. My pussy clenched. I parted my lips to try to say something, but nothing could come out, except more spit and a sloppy, wet gagging sound.

He slapped my pussy harder, and I gagged again. The guard pulled his cock out of me, and I gasped for breath. Cristian wrapped both his hands around my neck, forcing me to look at him. "You don't want to know what happens if you make me ask it again."

"You," I breathed out. "You, sir."

He nodded and loosened his grip on my neck. One hand wandered down my body to my pussy, and he plunged a finger into it. I immediately clenched around him, my pussy desperate for anything to be inside of it right now.

"Are you ever going to betray me again?" he asked.

He stuck another finger inside of me, and I shook my head.

"No, sir." My pussy tightened even more.

"What do you say when you want something from now on?" he asked.

"Please," I said.

"And what do you want now?"

My heart raced. He knew exactly what I wanted—for him to fuck me.

"For you to put your cock inside of me," I said.

He roughly brushed his thumb over my lip, tilting my head to the side.

"Please, sir," I said, gazing up at him through my lashes.

He undid his belt, pushed the head of his cock against my wet pussy, and then shoved himself inside of me.

My pussy tightened around him, shaping to his size. He groaned, eyes closing.

"Principessa, I've been waiting for you to fuck up for so long." He grasped my thighs, holding them apart, and pumped into me slowly. One of his hands slid down my thigh, and he harshly rubbed my clit, pumping faster into me.

The pressure already started to build in my throat, and I curled my toes, letting them use me. I loved it so fucking much. I couldn't even think about anything that just happened. Just him and them and the heat in my core.

His fingers moved quicker around my swollen clit, my juices getting on them. Marco grasped my breasts from behind and squeezed both of my nipples between his fingers. My body jerked up into the air, and I screamed out as the pleasure pumped out of me.

My legs shook in Cristian's hands, yet he didn't stop thrusting into me. Instead, he pumped harder and faster, giving me every-thing he had. And, fuck, he had a lot. One of the guards thrust his cock into my mouth and all the way down my throat, pumping in and out of me.

Cristian wrapped his hand around my throat. "Scream for me, Principessa."

I parted my lips, screaming as loud as I could with his guard's cock in my mouth. The man curled his fingers into my hair, using my head to thrust in and out. Cristian moved his fingers faster again, his hand tightening around my throat even more.

"Are you going to come again?"

I furrowed my brows and nodded, spit dripping down my chin. He slapped one of my tits hard with his hand, and I came undone again.

Marco stilled under me and pulled out of me, his cum dripping out of my ass.

Cristian grabbed me by the arm, forced me onto my knees, and pushed his cock down my throat. "Taste yourself," he said.

I gazed at him through my lashes, my full lips wrapping around his cock. Then, I sucked off all my juices. He groaned, stilling inside of me, then slowly pulled out, his warm cum dripping off my lips and onto my tits.

He smirked down at me, pulled up his pants, and redid his belt. "Mine."

Part 2

I leaned across the table at Cristian's club, sipped the last of my white wine, and smiled at my gorgeous date for the night. Dark and luscious locks, lovely brown eyes, and a smirk that nearly killed me, he leaned closer to me and placed his hand on my knee.

Since that bastard, Cristian, killed my ex-boyfriend in a rage and fucked me senseless next to his dead body, I decided to stay the fuck away from him. And by that, I really meant, get on his every last nerve until he fucked me that way again.

I had been on countless dates with countless men at his club, but the guys were all driven away quite quickly. No, *not by me*. But by the security team who Cristian gave his orders to. I was angry that it wasn't him doing it himself, but I knew it was getting to him.

All I had to do was push a little bit harder.

My date for tonight said something in Italian to me, which I couldn't understand, nor could I hear it over this loud music. So, I just happily nodded and brushed my fingers against his forearm, knowing that Cristian was watching us from across the bar.

As my date continued to talk nonsense to me, thoughts raced through my head about what Cristian would do to me the next time I broke him. Tug on my hair. Run his hands all over my body. Take me however he wanted. He touched me like he owned me, and he did after my ex decided to drag me into his stupid escape plan.

Every inch of my body was Cristian's, and him not even touching me annoyed the fuck out of me. I sat up straight, pushed out my breasts, and smiled. But not tonight. Tonight, I was going to break him. I didn't care what I had to do. Flirt, push my hand down this guy's pants in the middle of the club, fuck him in Cristian's bed. I didn't give a shit. I'd do it.

My core warmed, lips curling into a smile as I thought about the last option.

That'd definitely fuck with Cristian enough.

I grabbed the guy's hand, completely forgetting his name, made sure that Cristian saw us leaving, and pulled him out of the club, down the block, and into a luxurious apartment building. I might've stolen a key to Cristian's high-rise the other day for things like this. He never used the place, only when he was at the club for the night, so I thought it'd be nice to sleep in his bed instead of the shitty apartment my ex had me living in.

I was almost certain that Cristian knew about it, as he'd mentioned it a couple times, looking directly at me and waiting for me to fess up to him. But I sealed my lips. I wasn't going to willingly give the key up to him. He'd have to take it back from me.

As we rode the elevator to the top floor, my date kissed my neck, his hands traveling down my body, up my inner thigh—touching me in places that I only wanted Cristian to touch me. When the doors opened, I stuck my key into the lock and walked into Cristian's apartment.

Whatever his name was stared around with wide eyes. "This is where you live?" he asked me in a thick Italian accent.

I didn't want him asking any more questions. I knew Cristian was probably out looking for me by now, so I nodded and pushed him to the back bedroom.

From floor to ceiling, two of the walls were complete windows, overlooking the city. I pushed him back onto the bed and climbed on top of him, unbuttoning his shirt as quickly as I could. He mumbled something to me, which I didn't understand, and groped my ass, squeezing it in his hands.

When I heard the apartment door open, my heart raced in my chest. I kissed him harder, hoping that he didn't hear it, and flipped us over so I was under him. Grabbing the waistband of my skirt, he pulled it down and left me in my underwear, his eyes lingering on my wet panties.

But they weren't wet because of him. They were wet because of

…

Cristian stormed into the room, grabbed the guy by the back of the neck, and tore him off me. "This is really how you want to fucking play with me, Principessa?" he asked me, the vein in his neck pulsing wildly. He shoved him against the wall, his hand around the man's throat, squeezing so tightly. "What's his fucking name?"

I scrambled up to the headboard, my heart racing in my chest. "I don't know."

Cristian chuckled menacingly at me. "You think you could just bring him up here and fuck him in my bed to make me angry?" he asked. "You want to be a fucking whore like every other woman in this family?"

I pressed my lips together and glared at him. "I'm not a whore," I said through gritted teeth. "And I don't want to be part of this family. I never wanted to be part of this fucking family."

He thrust the man into the wall harder and turned back to me. The guy tried to make a run for it, but Cristian put a hand on his chest and pushed him toward the window.

"You, stay," he said through clenched teeth. "I'll fucking deal with you later."

The man looked absolutely terrified, his eyes wide, sweat dripping down the side of his neck. It was pitiful. I had known exactly what was going to happen to him when I brought him home tonight. Truth was, I chose him carefully, saw him dropping pills in a girl's drink, knew he'd do anything to get a woman alone. And later, he'd die for it.

Cristian turned back to me and stepped closer to the bed. "I don't care if you want to be in this fucking family or not," he said, grasping my ankle and yanking me to the edge of the bed. He snatched my jaw in his hand and forced me to look up at him, drawing his thumb roughly across my bottom lip. "I own you. You betrayed me. You're part of this family until I tell you you're not." He menacingly glared at me.

"I don't understand you," he said to me, hand slipping around my throat. "Do you want me to treat you like a whore? Or is it that you just want my attention and want me to fuck you senseless again?"

I swallowed hard, my pussy clenching.

He tugged me closer to him. "That's what you've been begging for, isn't it?" he asked.

I furrowed my brows and gnawed on the inside of my cheek.

"How many times have you played with this pretty pussy in my bed, thinking about me?" He slid his hand between my legs and started to rub my clit.

I let out a low whimper, my legs starting to shake.

"How many fucking times?" he asked into my ear, fingers moving faster.

"Every night for the past two weeks," I whispered.

He curled his hand around the hem of my panties and ripped them right off of me. "You couldn't stop thinking about me, could you?" He stuffed my panties into my mouth. "Turn around, ass in the air, face against the mattress, looking back at me."

My eyes widened slightly, and when I didn't move, he pushed me back onto the bed. I turned around, sat on my knees with my ass in the air, and gazed back at him, just as he wanted me to. He grasped the zipper on the front of my shirt and pulled it down to let my breasts bounce out of it.

Pulling my arms behind my back, he slapped my ass hard, whipped out his cock, and rubbed it against my entrance. "Look at me," Cristian said. "Nowhere else. You keep your eyes on me the entire time I fuck you, or there will be consequences, Principessa."

I curled my toes and nodded, the panties still in my mouth.

"Arch your back."

He rested his hand on my lower back, and I waited for him to enter me. I felt the tip of his head rub against my wetness, and my pussy clenched. He continued to rub against my pussy, not entering me, then slapped it roughly against my clit, making me moan. A wave of pleasure coursed through my body.

He snaked a hand around the back of my neck to hold me down, placed a foot on the bed, and rammed his big cock into my tight pussy. He stared down at me, strands of his thick brown hair on his forehead, never once taking his eyes off me. My legs shook in pleasure as he wrapped his arm around my waist and began to rub circles around my clit.

Moaning loudly from the pleasure building in my core, I clenched around him. "Harder," I breathed.

He slammed into me harder, burying his dick as deep as it would go.

God, I loved this too much, too fucking much.

I furrowed my brows together, my legs already beginning to shake. He grasped my waist, thumbs pressing into my abdomen, and drew me closer to him. I could feel his balls hitting my pussy, his hips hitting against my clit.

I was going to come. I was going to—

Pressure built up in my core, and I whimpered. Unable to handle it any longer. He slammed himself into me one last time and relaxed inside of me, his cum dripping out of my pussy and down my thighs. He pulled me up to a kneeling position by the hair.

"He's dead," he said into my ear. "Nobody touches you unless I say they can." He stood up, tossed me a silk robe, and grabbed one of his many guns hidden in this room from his nightstand.

The man shuffled away until his back was against the wall, shaking his head and looking terrified. "No, please, no … I didn't do anything," he said in that thick accent.

Cristian pulled me off the bed. "You're my girl," he said. He grabbed my hand, wrapped it around the gun, and forced me to hold it to my date's head. "So, you're going to kill him, take his life. He's betrayed me. Touched what's mine."

"Me?" I asked almost breathlessly.

I was damn fine with watching him do it … but me? I couldn't … I …

"This is punishment for trying to run away from me," he said into my ear, smacking my pussy hard with his hand. "I do what I want with you, and you love it, don't you?"

I nodded, my breath hitched in the back of my throat.

"Good. Look him in the eye when you do it, Principessa." He paused. "Show me that I can trust you again. Show me that I don't have to kill you too. I know there was a reason you brought him back here with you, other than to piss me off. I know that you wanted me to kill him for you. But if you want this, if you want me, if you want to be the boss's girl, you will kill him without a second thought."

To be his girl …

I took a deep breath and pulled the trigger.

Anything to be his one and only.

These one-shots have been turned into a book. Read Mafia Boss now!

mafia gangbanger

"RICCI, YOU GOT A VISITOR."

My cell door clicked open, and Stan stood outside with a gun on his hip and cuffs in his hands. He cocked a finger in my direction and motioned for me to hold out my wrists. After cursing at him, I held out my hands and let him snap the silver cuffs around them.

Could I kill him if I wanted? Sure. Would it get me out of this shithole any faster? Fuck no. It had been four long years in this hell already, and I didn't want to make it a fucking lifetime without getting back out there with my family.

"Who is it?" I asked, walking down the long corridors with him to a separate room.

Instead of answering me, Stan opened the door to the visitation facility. I took one look into the busy room and grunted. "Fuck me," I mumbled, walking to the table with my lawyer and taking a seat in front of him. "What do you want this fucking time?"

Dressed in a black suit that my family's money paid for, John cracked a smile. "I have something for you."

"The only thing I fucking need is for you to get me the fuck out of here," I said between clenched teeth. My hands were bound in thick silver cuffs that I had worn for the past four years and would wear for at least the next three if he didn't do something about it.

John readjusted his suit jacket and blew out a breath. "You're part of the Ricci Family, Mateo, the biggest crime family in New York. They're not going to turn a blind eye to what you did, no matter the amount of money the family tries to bribe them with."

After vowing that I'd get a better lawyer next time, one who knew how to do his fucking job, I sat back. "What do you got for me, because if it's just this shitty conversation, I'd like to go back to my cell?"

Sticking his hand into his suit pocket, he pulled out a white envelope and slid it across the metal table toward me. I eyed it, glancing between him and the mail that had a return address to somewhere in Texas but no name.

"Who sent this to you?" I asked.

"It showed up in my office this morning from a fake address in Texas, the same address as the last few of your care packages. Do you know who it could be from?" A low chuckle escaped his lips. "Because they're awfully *generous*."

"Generous?" I asked, pushing my finger into the white envelope and ripping it open.

Tilting the envelope upside down, a picture slid out and into my hand. It was of a woman biting her lip, red curls framing her breasts, finger hooked around the hem of her shirt between her cleavage. Though her eyes were just outside the scope of the camera, I couldn't forget a body like hers.

Eliza Lewis.

I curled my lips into a smile.

Eliza fucking Lewis, the girl who my gangbanger family scared away, the girl I broke up with a month before the FBI swarmed my house, the only girl I ever fucking loved had been sending me packages for the past few years. Now, I receive a picture.

She was a tease, and she fucking knew it.

"Do you know her?" John said.

Flipping the picture over, I cut my gaze to John. "Did you fucking jerk off to this?"

John tense and shook his head. "It's your picture."

"That didn't answer my question. Now, did. You. Jerk. Off. To. This?"

"No," John finally said.

I clenched my jaw and sat back in the seat. "If I find out that you did, I'll chop your fucking balls off with a machete when I get out of here. Next time she sends me anything, don't comment on it and don't open it. She's for my eyes only."

John loosened his tie and drew his tongue across his teeth, the way he always did when nervous. After sitting back up, he looked around the room. "Hide it, before a guard comes over and takes it from you. You know how strict they are around here. Nobody's watching."

Once I hid the picture away, I cleared my throat. "You understand me? No opening her shit. She's mine."

"I've never heard you speak about anyone before."

After standing up, I nodded to Stan. "We're done here."

John leaned closer. "You're not going to–"

Stan grabbed my elbow and pulled me to the exit. I clenched my jaw, walking all the way back to my cell and thanking god when he took those fucking cuffs off my wrists. I hated it here even more now that I knew Eliza was still thinking about me.

I hopped onto my bunk, pulled out the picture of Eliza, and spit on my hand. After shoving a hand into my pants, I blew out a deep breath and stroked my cock, getting harder and harder by the damn second at the thought of Eliza, *my Eliza*, getting so horny for me that she snapped a picture of herself and mailed it to my lawyer for me.

My hand moved up and down my shaft, tightening as much as Eliza used to when she rode me, her nails digging into my taut chest, tracing my tattoos, full lips parted in delight and sexy little whimpers escaping her mouth.

Grunting, I moved my hips up and down, imaging pushing myself into Eliza's mouth, her cheeks drawn in, head bobbing back and forth and tongue swirling around my head. Pushing a strand of her natural curly ginger hair behind her ear. Making her cheeks flush red and her spit coat her lips.

Closing my eyes, I imagined the night I realized that she would love me for even my faults, the night I had drove to her cop ex-husband's house, smashed all his windows in so the glass littered the floor, strangled him to death in his sleep, and set fire to his cottage in the woods that he used to take her to and rape her.

We fucked in my car as the flames danced across the sky that night, a blazing orange sunrise that Eliza told me that she had forgotten about before I got put away, but that was a lie. I had watched her smile every time we passed the station that he used to work at.

"Fuck," I drew out, stroking my cock up and down, hard and fast. I pulled up the bottom of my shirt and came onto my stomach. Unable to hold myself back, I groaned out loud and didn't give a fuck who heard it. My Eliza wanted me back, and when I got out of here, she would be the first person I paid a visit to take her back, make her *mine* again.

want more steamy shorts?

I write new one-shots every week (including some new mafia stories)! They're only available on Ream.

also by emilia rose

Scan the QR code with your phone to view all of Emilia's books!

also by emilia rose

Contemporary Romance

Stepbrother

Poison

The Bad Boy

Detention

Excite Me

Paranormal Romance

Submitting to the Alpha

Come Here, Kitten

Alpha Maddox

My Werewolf Professor

The Twins

Four Masked Wolves

Monster Lover

Erotica

Climax: Erotic One-Shot Collection

about the author

Emilia Rose is a USA Today best-selling author of steamy romance. Highly inspired by her study abroad trip to Greece in 2019, Emilia loves to include Greek and Roman mythology in her writing.

She graduated from the University of Pittsburgh with a degree in psychology and a minor in creative writing in 2020 and now writes novels as her day job.

With over 18 million combined book views online and a growing presence on reading apps, she hopes to inspire other young novelists with her tales of growth and imagination, so they go on to write the stories that need to be told.

Join Emilia's newsletter for exclusive giveaways, early chapter releases, and more!

9 781954 597846